Hearts in the Storm

Elmer Seward

Bay Rivers Publishing

ISBN-10: 0692234497

ISBN-13: 978-0692234495

Cover design created utilizing Shutterstock AI Image Generator

The most destructive storm rages within the heart.

Chapter 1

He dragged himself out of the seaside door onto the long, wooden deck. Standing for a moment, he watched the waves whipping up foam as they battered the beleaguered sand. The surging water spewed shells and rocks along the shoreline only to snatch them up, like secrets dredged from the deep, in its frantic retreat. The sea was in constant motion. There was an offshore storm, and the beach was catching the brunt of its fury.

He took a long, slow sip of coffee, hoping to clear the cluttered remnants of last night's bender. Wearing only a tattered pair of shorts, he peered out beneath hooded brows toward the gray and ominous horizon. Even this thickly filtered daylight hurt, as he studied the churning sea.

Laying his cup on the railing, he leaned forward, straining to glimpse the pelicans riding the rolling waves just beyond the break. They'd appear as they crested the top of the swells and then disappear as they slid down into the troughs. Occasionally, one would take flight, circle briefly, and then dive, disappearing beneath the water for a brief moment.

As he watched, something odd caught his attention. Just beyond the birds, another dark object in the water appeared and disappeared in the rolling waves. At first, he thought it might be one of the sea birds, but there was something unusual about the shape. Maybe it was a fin. It was common to see dolphins just offshore. It could be a shark fin. They prowled the shoreline more often than the local tourist companies wanted to announce. It crested into view again. No, it was too far out and in the sunless water, too dark to identify but not a fin. It disappeared again. He watched closely, waiting for it to crest. There it was, but it was taller. It was moving. It was an arm. A head and waving arm tossed and swallowed up in the tumultuous water.

The thundering sound of the waves, roaring and crashing, was all consuming, but faintly, he heard another sound, almost imperceptible. It was a voice in the intermittent roar and crash, a voice crying for help.

He glanced up and down the beach. There was no one else to help. He had to act quickly. Grabbing an old cork safety ring that hung as a decorative prop on the deck, he leaped down the steps to the beach. As he ran, his feet sank into the loose, shifting sand. It felt like he was lifting leaden legs as he struggled forward. Finally reaching the firmer wet sand, he sped up only to hit the water. Again, each step was like dragging an anvil. He pressed forward into the waves, diving into each one to avoid being knocked backward. As he wrestled in the rush and the roar, he searched desperately to find the person who'd rise and then vanish in the rolling action of the ocean.

Swimming now, fighting against the current determined to rush him back to shore, he was becoming exhausted. The water battered and pulled at him, but he pressed on, trailing the safety ring in his wake.

He was close now. He could see the figure, a girl, maybe in her teens. She flailed her arms, desperately fighting to keep her head above water. She was losing the battle. Alternately, she choked, gasped, and screamed as her head broke the water… only to be sucked down again.

As he swam within feet of the struggling figure, the girl disappeared. He searched the waves that crashed around him. There was no sign of the girl. He dove hoping to find her. The dark, churning water was murky and obscured his vision. Then he saw a hand just below him. He swam deeper, his lungs burning. Now, her face emerged from the darkness. Her eyes were wide with panic as her outstretched fingers clawed desperately. One more stroke propelled him downward. He stretched out to grasp her flailing hands. His fingers were inches away. In the next instant, she was swept away in the shifting current. He peered through the darkness, his lungs about to burst. She was gone.

Chapter 2

He was wet and gasping for air. Darkness enveloped him as he sat upright in his bed. Desperately, he tried to grasp the safety float of reality in the churning sea of his nightmare. Sleep – where others found rest and peace, he found fitful nights of terror. The violent water, the exhausting struggle, the panicked, drowning girl, his dismal failure… all haunted him in sleepless nights. The setting and other details of this dark dream would change from time to time, but in the end, he always saw the panic in her eyes just before she slipped from his grasp.

He was too shaken to consider sleep. He looked at the clock, 4:00 a.m. He sat for a while, trying to calm his nerves. Eventually, he shuffled wearily to the refrigerator, grabbed two bottles of beer, and then shuffled out to the deck.

Plopping down into the heavy wooden deck chair, he sat, looking out at the ocean. Unlike his dream, the waves gently washed in, lingered and then slipped out. The large, full moon hovering on the horizon cast a web of dancing, glistening shards on the water. He watched the light show as he methodically sipped his beer. The monotonous lapping of the waves on the sand, the sparkling play of moonlight on the water, and the sedative of the alcohol worked their magic. Soon he was asleep.

*   *   *

"Duck! Hey, Duck!"

Like a man coming out of a coma, he struggled to put the pieces together. He heard his name. He saw the white-hot sun burning a hole in the blue sky. He felt a stabbing pain that shot up the back of his neck and exploded in his brain, his head bent back at an unnatural angle. Where was he?

"Duck!"

He shook his head, trying to make all the pieces fall into place.

"Are you OK?"

Through very groggy eyes, he made out the blurry figure of his sister standing below him on the stairs leading up from the beach. The gears still weren't meshing inside his brain.

"What'd you say?" Duck looked lost as he stood unsteadily.

"Oh, good grief!" His sister grimaced as she glanced away. "Get some clothes on!"

He looked down. He stood on the deck in nothing but a faded pair of ripped Fruit of the Looms. Gaping holes in the worn fabric revealed more than they hid. He glanced up to find an attractive woman walking the shore just beyond his sister. She wore a lightweight, neon pink jacket and white shorts. Hearing his sister's exclamation, she turned their direction and was now staring at Duck. Her gaze followed him as she passed with an "I can't believe this idiot" look on her face. He weakly waved with one hand as he attempted to cover a particularly troublesome rip with the other.

"Mornin'," he called out.

She grimaced as she turned her head back toward the shoreline. Looking up at the sky, he pounded his forehead with the palm of his hand and then winced from the eruption of pain in his head. His sister burst out laughing.

Duck glared at her. "Thanks!" He said as he turned toward the cottage door.

"You're the genius sleeping in the deck chair in that ratty underwear. It's not my fault."

Duck peered down the beach at the disappearing pink jacket to make sure the woman wasn't looking. Hooking his thumbs in the rear waistband of his Fruit of the Looms, he pulled down far enough to flash a pale half-moon that stood out in contrast to his tanned torso. Quickly, he released, and the waistband snapped back just before he stepped inside.

"Duck!" As he disappeared through the screen door, his sister yelled after him, "Hey, I've seen better."

She could hear his laughter echoing from the kitchen. She climbed the stairs and sat in one of the chairs, looking out at the deserted beach. Tourist season was over. Kids were back in school. For a few months, the little beach town could exhale and recover, only locals and an occasional older couple visiting. No more summer frantic rush.

Duck emerged through the screen door, white t-shirt with a faded beer logo and khaki shorts now in place. He carried two bottles of beer in his hand. Scooting the two empties from last night to the side, he set the cold beer on the small table between him and his sister.

Her gaze shifted from the shore to her brother. Her eyes narrowed. "A little early in the day for drinking, don't you think?"

Looking out at the water, Duck shrugged, lifted one of the bottles to his lips, and took a long sip.

She stared at her brother with no response. Finally, she said, "I just thought that I'd see how you're doing before I slipped off to work. You were in pretty bad shape last night. You kept calling me 'Mommy.'"

Duck looked sheepish and just chuckled.

"Look, I know I probably changed your diaper as often as mom did, but still, that's just weird. From what I saw this morning, I guess I had reason to worry."

Duck looked over. Her face was hard. He and his sister joked a lot, but she was all business now.

"Look, Sissy, I'm good. You don't need to worry about me so much."

The stern look continued. "Duck, when are you going to come out of this funk? I miss my brother."

He looked at the bottle of beer and swirled the liquid around, studying it, seemingly lost in the motion.

"Duck!"

"What?" His eyes snapped up to meet hers.

"I said, 'I miss you.'"

He sighed as he gazed out at the water. "I'm right here… every day… right here."

Sissy sighed, tapped her fingers on the table, and then shifted the conversation. "Have you been watching that storm blowing up in the Atlantic?"

Duck's gaze drifted back to her. "Not really. I don't pay attention to that stuff anymore."

Sissy snapped back, "Well, you better start paying attention to it! You live on the beach!" She took a breath, then exhaled to calm herself. "The forecast shows us dead in the center of the projected path. It's big and getting stronger. I'm worried."

Duck squinted out at the ocean as if he were looking for the distant storm. "When is it supposed to hit?"

Sissy shook her head. "You know these things. Right now, they think Thursday, but it could speed up or slow down."

Duck nodded, continuing to peer out at the ocean as if mesmerized.

Sissy broke the spell. "If they call a mandatory evacuation, I'm leaving. Will you come with me?"

"Nah, I'll probably just ride out the storm here in the old beach bunker." He motioned toward the cottage.

Sissy blew hot again. "Do you remember what some of these houses looked like after Hurricane Isabel? This isn't a fortress. It's a pile of neatly arranged straw waiting for the big, bad wolf!"

Duck chuckled which infuriated Sissy even more. She sat and fumed quietly. Picking up the other bottle from the table, she swigged down a big gulp of beer and launched into another sore subject.

"Cap tells me that you missed work again yesterday."

Duck studied his beer again as he swirled it. "Well, it was Saturday, and I felt like I'd already put in a full week—"

"Duck, you're going to lose your job! What are you going to do then?" She took in a deep breath to steady her voice. "Cap is probably the only person around who's willing to hire you. He's only doing it out of the goodness of his heart, but goodness only lasts so long." She watched as he continued to study the swirling beer. "He wanted me to tell you he needs you to come in at noon today. Please promise me that you'll show up."

Duck glared at his sister. "And you wonder why I called you 'Mommy' when I was drunk last night. Listen to you!"

Like the collision of a cold front and a tropical depression, a storm was about to blow. Sissy took a swallow of beer and clattered the half-empty bottle onto the table. She stood just inches in front of Duck, blocking his view of the ocean. "Fine, I can't help you if you aren't willing to try! You're a big boy. I guess you'll figure it out." She threw open the screen door letting it slam behind her. Duck could hear her stomping her way through the cottage punctuated by the crash of the front door.

The cottages on this little stretch of beach were built closer than most to the tall dunes that ran parallel to the shore. As a result, their seaside decks extended onto the dunes. This gave them an unobstructed view of the beach. As Duck watched the listless waves, a flash of neon pink from the corner of his eye caught his attention. The attractive woman was strolling back up the beach. She had dark hair cut just around the jawline. It framed her face beautifully. She was slender and shapely, almost athletic, but not severely thin or rugged.

As she passed the cottage, she looked over to the deck. Duck stood and grabbed the sides of his t-shirt between the forefinger and thumb of each hand and pulled on it to indicate his wardrobe change. Then he gave her a thumbs up and grinned. Her expression was sour as turned away.

Duck shrugged, sat down, and sipped his beer as he watched her rear end disappearing down the beach. *Not bad*, he thought.

He noticed the deck railing that now blocked his view of her rear. It was missing one of the vertical spokes. Several spaces away, another was hanging at an awkward angle. The entire deck was beginning to crack and splinter, and a few of the floorboards were warped. The exterior of the old, small cottage was weathered with missing shake shingles and showed years of exposure to the sun, the salt air, and neglect. Duck frowned as he took inventory of all that needed to be done. His mother wouldn't have been happy. When she passed away, leaving the cottage to Duck and Sissy, it was in good condition and well-maintained. Duck hadn't done much since that time and it showed. The inside of the cottage wasn't much better, but it was mostly clutter. Sissy's room was neat, and she tried to keep the rest of the house straight, but any place where Duck spent time looked like the path of a hurricane. It hadn't always been that way, but when Duck's life blew apart, he and the debris landed here with his sister. He and the place had been a mess ever since. Sissy tried to be understanding and patient, but sometimes her patience meter hit the red zone and she'd blow. Duck would calmly take the brunt of the explosion, give her a sheepish, *I'm sorry*, look, and then continue without much change. She couldn't stay mad at him for long.

As he sat thinking about all that needed to be done, he considered taking care of some of it. Then he thought, *maybe later*. Satisfied that he had a plan, he took another swig of beer.

An old golden retriever ambled onto the deck and flopped at Duck's feet as if the effort of pushing through the screen door had worn him out. Duck ran his foot over the dog's back and cooed, "Hey, old boy, you need to pace yourself. Don't want to wear yourself out this early in the day." He winked at the dog and smiled.

The little, one-story cottage was nestled in the middle of larger two-story rental properties. As long as Duck could remember, this had been his home. Where other boys had neighborhood friends, Duck had weekly visitors. Occasionally, he would make friends with tourist children visiting for a week, but the friendships were short lived. Mostly, his summers consisted of watching a different set of strangers come and go each week. The winters were spent with occasional visitors, but usually they were couples without children. Most of the time, he had the beach to himself.

He looked up the shoreline. The woman in the pink jacket was headed back toward him. He watched as she turned and climbed the steps leading to the cottage next door. So, she was his next-door neighbor… for a week. She had slender, tan legs, and Duck continued to study her. When she pushed at the door, it didn't budge, and she ran into it unexpectedly. She backed off, looking surprised. She grabbed the doorknob again and pushed unsuccessfully. Duck watched, amused, as she continued without much luck.

He stood up, stretched, and hopped down the stairs. The old dog loped along behind him. As he arrived at the woman's steps, she was rattling the door in frustration, cursing under her breath.

"Here, let me see if I can get that for you." He smiled, nodding toward the door as he climbed the steps.

She looked annoyed but stepped aside to give him a shot at the door. He laid his bottle of beer on the deck railing, grabbed the doorknob with his right hand, and jiggled it, watching for the location of the sticking point.

The woman grumbled, "I already tried that."

Duck smiled back. "These old wooden doors swell in the humidity and get stuck like this all the time." He found the sticking point about at eye level. As he jiggled the door, he slapped it at the sticking point with the flat of his left palm. It popped open.

Duck grinned and motioned with his hand as if he were ushering her inside. "There you go."

He grabbed his bottle of beer and stood there grinning for an uncomfortable moment. Finally, the woman grudgingly said, "Thanks."

Suddenly, Duck blurted, "Oh! Where are my manners?" He shifted the bottle from his right hand to his left, wiped his wet palm on his t-shirt, and extended it. "I'm Duck."

The woman left his extended hand hovering for a moment, eyeing it as if it were diseased. Reluctantly, she took his hand and quickly released it. "Trista," she said flatly.

A little late, Duck noticed the old dog wandering through the open door. "Fetch, get out here! Fetch!" The dog plopped on the floor inside. Duck stepped through the doorway and coaxed the dog up and back out onto the deck.

"I'm sorry. He's an old dog and gets confused sometimes. He gets lost easy 'cause his cataracts make it hard to see." The dog was wandering around on the deck. Duck commanded, "Fetch, sit!" The dog sat.

Duck motioned toward the dog. "This is Fetch." He waited for a response.

Trista returned a blank stare.

"Get it? Retriever, Fetch?" Duck grinned.

Trista wasn't amused. "Got it. Duck and Fetch." She'd had enough. "OK, well, thanks for getting the door open." She flashed a faint smile and stepped inside the doorway.

Duck called after her, "Any time. If you need anything, I'm…" The door shut. "… right next door."

Duck stood for a moment grinning at the closed door. Then his smile disappeared as he nodded in acceptance. Heading down the steps, he called back, "Come on, boy." The old dog ambled down the stairs and loped along beside him. Duck reached down and ruffled the dog's coat. "You noticed it too, didn't you, old boy?" Duck smiled but his voice was weary. "Yeah, she's totally into me." Together they walked along the shoreline of a calm, sunlit ocean, but Duck's storm-tossed nightmares were never far beyond the horizon.

Chapter 3

Exhaling, Trista collapsed onto the closed door, spent from struggling against the undertow that had become her life. Moments later, recovering, she stood and peered out the side window. Just across the sandy way, Duck lounged on his deck, sipping his bottle of beer. Fetch was stretched out contentedly at his feet. Just this brief encounter had stressed and exhausted her. She thought that she was better, stronger. That was the whole reason that she made this trip. Now, she wasn't sure that this was a good idea. She peeked out at Duck again. If he cleaned up his ragged hair and trimmed or shaved his beard, he would be a good-looking man. Even worse, he was like a frat boy trapped in a grown man's body. He appeared to be in his mid to late thirties, but there he was, the sun barely up, drinking like he was on a liquid diet.

Trista longed to sun on the deck and listen to the hypnotic rhythm of the waves lapping on the shore, but she couldn't stand the thought of suffering the smiles and waves and who knows what other antics from the neighbor lounging next door. She grudgingly settled for opening one of the seaside windows and reclining in an overstuffed chair. As she watched the gulls circle above the deserted beach, she grew angry. Why did he have to be so childish? Men! Mesmerized by the steady ebb and flow of the waves, she gazed into the distance. Not the distance measured in miles, but the distance measured in years, to an earlier, more tumultuous time.

* * *

Trista stood in the doorway, screaming out as he loaded the last suitcase in the trunk.

"It's not safe! Change your plans!" Angry tears streamed down her face.

He slammed the trunk and grinned. "You're overreacting. You always blow things way out of proportion."

She shot back, "No. You never take anything seriously. You joke and play things down. You run from responsibility and make fun of anyone who questions your childish behavior. When are you going to grow up?"

He looked up just before sliding into the driver's seat. "Well, we can't all be terminally serious like you. Give it a rest. Things'll be fine."

The car door slammed. She sobbed as the car drove off.

*   *   *

Engulfed by the overstuffed chair as if in a cocoon, tears streaked her face. He had been wrong that day several years ago. Everything didn't turn out fine. Regretting this trip, she realized she had also been wrong. She really wasn't better.

Inside her cottage, inside her heart, under dark stormy clouds, the past raged and crashed. Waves of regret, anger, and pain battered her soul. Outside in the sparkling sun, the waves gently caressed the beach as the gulls glided overhead.

Chapter 4

Sissy was still raging hot as she jerked the steering wheel of the old jeep and scattered gravel, swerving into the parking lot in front of *The One That Got Away Café*. She slumped into the seat, exhausted from the rage and the sorrow. She was tired of fighting, tired of being the unsuccessful mother to a grown brother. Angry tears streamed down her face. She loved Duck. With both of their parents gone, he was her only real family. Over the past few years, she'd helplessly stood by him as he shut out the world, Sissy included. He built a wall of drunken carelessness that he hid behind. Sissy sobbed as tears of frustration continued to pour. She wanted so badly to help him but didn't know how. Her frustration always led to anger. She'd blow up in Duck's face. He'd just shrug it off as if he were a detached bystander. But she knew that it hurt him deep where no one could see. Then the anger led to regret for not being more understanding. She was exhausted. She felt like giving up and then felt guilty for feeling that way. Sissy sat for a long while, swiping at the tears as she tried to compose herself.

She glanced at her reflection in the rearview mirror and thought of how she looked like a dry riverbed. The tears, now gone, left behind only the ugly, dry dirt bed. She looked tired and empty. She took a moment to apply a little makeup, but it only partly masked her exhaustion. Sissy took a deep breath. "Life must go on," she muttered to her reflection and then exited the car.

As she pushed through the café door to the aroma of brewing coffee and tea, a big, round man behind the bar called out playfully, "You're late, Em." He smiled.

She frowned.

"Can you get the silverware out on the tables?"

Her name was Emma, but her friends called her Em. Only Duck and his friends called her Sissy. Duck, for the obvious reason, and his friends, because it was all they ever heard him call her.

She took a few steps and froze, mesmerized by the spinning orange and yellow pinwheel on the TV screen above the bar. The round man noticed, looked up at the screen, and whistled. "That's a monster of a storm." The jerky nature of the time-lapse movement gave it an eerie appearance. Sissy shook her head. The meteorologist, superimposed over a map of the east coast, was dwarfed by the huge storm. The Outer Banks were in the dead center of its projected path. The tiny man on the screen used terms like, "storm of the century," and, "widespread destruction." And there they were, the little barrier islands, dangling out in the ocean like tempting bait on a hook, waiting for this monster to strike.

Sissy spoke, still hypnotized by the spinning buzz saw on the screen. "If they call for a mandatory evacuation, are you leaving, Jimbo?"

The big man looked up at the TV screen again. "Only a crazy person would stay here with that bearing down on them." He looked back at Sissy. "How about you?"

Sissy said, "I'm outa here."

"How about Duck?" Jimbo's eyes narrowed.

She shook her head. "He says he's staying."

Jimbo shook his head. "Like I said, only a crazy person."

A sad smile crept across Sissy's face. She knew that Jimbo was mostly joking. Jimbo liked Duck. He was one of the few people around who did. But he only said what most others thought. Common consensus was that Duck was off in the head. Maybe not crazy in the classic sense of the term, but people thought he just wasn't right. Unfortunately, Duck didn't do much to discourage that perception.

Sissy went about the morning preparation for lunch service, but her thoughts wandered through memories of childhood, a time when her brother was just that, an annoying younger brother. He was happy and had the whole world before him. Somewhere along the way, that had all come apart.

Jimbo's voice broke her somber mood. "Well, lookie there." Sissy glanced up to see Jimbo staring out the window to the parking lot. She followed his gaze. A TV remote satellite truck parked and three people spilled out into the sunlight. Jimbo spat out sarcastically, "Well, it's officially a hurricane party. Our foul-weather friends have arrived." It was a derogatory term he'd used for the TV crews that showed up any time a storm was predicted. Obviously, the expression "foul-weather friends" had multiple meanings in this context. He had great disdain for those who, on air, expressed concern for the poor communities in the path of the storm, but who, off air, salivated over the ratings that great destruction would bring.

The TV crew strode into the restaurant looking around like thieves casing their next heist. Jimbo called out, "We don't open 'til 11:00."

The young, handsome one, obviously the reporter, spoke without looking at Jimbo, "That's OK. We're just looking for a good place to set up for interviews. I think this place will do. It's got a real local, authentic feel."

If red check, plastic tablecloths, wood plank walls, beer advertising posters, and an odd collection of nautical memorabilia on the walls was local and authentic, then *The One That Got Away* had it.

The reporter pointed to a location near the bar. "We can set up over here—"

"I said we're not open yet."

The reporter shot back without looking, "Yeah, yeah, I get it."

Jimbo's anger grew. "No, you don't, so I'll make it simple. Get out!"

The reporter glanced up at Jimbo. "Now, there's no need to get upset. We'll stay out of the way and—"

"Out! Now!" Jimbo's face was a hot red as he slammed a mug on the bar and started toward the crew. They scrambled out the door.

He stood in the doorway and watched as they jumped into the van and sped out of the lot, kicking up gravel as they hit the highway. He turned back, anger still in his voice. "I'm not sure which is worse, the storm or the storm chasers."

Chapter 5

Trista stepped from the shower, wrapped a towel around her, and looked at the stranger in the mirror. There'd been a time when men told her that she was beautiful. She hadn't heard that in a long time. Her mother used to say, "Beauty is as beauty does." She sighed. That made two strikes against her. For the past few years, she hadn't been very good company. She'd become sullen, angry, and cold, and she knew it. She heard the names that coworkers called her when they didn't think she was listening. They'd been understanding at first, but over time, her harshness had worn thin. Earlier in her life, the whispered comments would have hurt, but now they just didn't matter.

She'd hoped that this trip to the shore would make a difference, bring back the old Trista. So far, things weren't looking good. She lightly touched the silver necklace that hung as a bright counterpoint against her dark, tanned neckline. It was half a heart with a jagged edge down the center. Her name was engraved on the smooth, shiny surface. She looked up from the necklace at the melancholy woman in the mirror. She hardly knew the person staring back at her.

Trista would only be at the shore for a few days. She needed to use the time that she had wisely. She set about taking care of the first piece of important business. She quickly dressed in a white, sleeveless blouse and a pair of dark khaki shorts. The collar of the blouse was open, revealing the small, silver necklace. It was after Labor Day, but the daytime temperatures on the coast were still warm and the sky was sunny. Trista grabbed her purse, fished out the car keys, and headed out the door.

She slid into the driver's seat of her car and drove up the narrow road through a claustrophobic mash of cottages and scrub brush. Turning onto

Highway 12, she headed toward a nearby marina. She'd noticed a small restaurant there as she drove past yesterday. It was lunchtime, and maybe she could get a line on a charter from someone there. She glanced at the clock on the dash, 11:10. They should be open. She swung the car into the gravel lot and parked near the café. Sundays were typically busy days at restaurants, but it was still early and only a few cars dotted the parking lot. The church crowd would probably be arriving soon.

The restaurant was a long, single-story building raised about eight feet above the gravel lot on haphazardly angled wooden pilings. The exterior was faded gray shake shingles. As Trista reached the wooden stairway, a small sign on a post next to the steps caught her eye. Against a white background, a horizontal red line ran just below red text that declared,

HIGH WATER MARK

HURRICANE IRENE

AUGUST 27, 2011

Trista paused as she read the sign. The red line fell just short of her chin. She'd seen the news reports and knew of the devastation, but this simple sign brought it all into focus in a much more powerful way.

Inside the restaurant were more sobering reminders of the dangers of living on this fragile strip of land. As she passed through the entrance, her attention was drawn to several photos on the wall. One showed a stretch of Highway 12, Hurricane Irene's teeth having ripped away several jagged sections of asphalt. Other photos graphically displayed homes shattered and splintered by the storm surge and winds. One revealed a torn and awkwardly tilting half of a dwelling with bare pilings jutting out of the sand where the other half once stood. Another showed a large boat lying on its side in a gravel parking lot and scattered debris ripped from docks strewn around it. The restaurant she now stood in was visible in the background of the photo. She thought of how the haunting photos closely paralleled the wreckage of her own storm-shattered life.

Startled by a booming voice calling out from the bar, "Come on in and have a seat," she noticed the *Please Be Seated* sign just beyond the entrance. A large man behind the bar was motioning to her. She picked out a table with a window view of the marina. Along the other wall of the restaurant ran a long bar that appeared to be constructed from various-sized pilings to give it a nautical look. The TV above the bar caught her attention. Meteorologists and reporters, each in turn, shared tales of past storms, their devastation, and the certain destruction that was to come. Trista watched, rapt in awe and fear. The awe was inspired by the sheer size of the storm. The fear wasn't of the storm but of how it might impact her trip and her plans. She hung on the words of the meteorologist, listening for any hopeful sign that the storm would change course. There was the possibility of a controlling high diving down from Canada and steering the storm farther out to sea, but it was a remote possibility at this point.

Trista was so caught up in the broadcast that she was startled when the waitress slid up from behind her. "Hi, my name's Emma. I'll be taking your order. Can I start you off with something to drink?"

Trista blinked for a second, speechless, as she tried to shift her attention from the TV to the unexpected waitress. "Well… I think I'll just have water." There was something about the waitress. She knew her from somewhere. The beach! That was it. She was the woman talking to Duck this morning as she walked the shoreline.

Emma smiled. "OK, I'll leave a menu for you to look over, and I'll be right back with your water. Lemon?"

Trista shook her head. "No thanks."

As Emma left to retrieve her water, Trista watched. She was about Trista's height with a very similar frame; however, she appeared to be older than Duck. It had been a very brief exchange, but the waitress seemed to be more responsible too. She just couldn't picture the two of them together. Trista didn't see any rings, so she must be his girlfriend, not his wife.

Trista shrugged and then turned to the menu. She loved seafood but only if it was fresh. She suspected that the food here would be just off the boat. There were plenty of great-looking options on the menu.

The waitress returned with a tall glass of ice water. "Have you decided what you'd like?"

Trista looked up from the menu. The waitress was an attractive woman, but, despite her smile, appeared to be weary. Trista knew the look well. It stared back at her from the mirror every day.

Pointing at an item on the menu, Trista asked, "How's the flounder stuffed with crab meat?"

Emma's face brightened a bit. "It's one of my favorites. The flounder and crab are all from local waters. It's prepared in a lightly seasoned butter sauce. Delicious."

It sounded great. Trista said, "I'll have that with the steamed broccoli."

Writing on her pad, the waitress asked, "Would you like a salad or appetizer with that?"

Trista shook her head. "No, that's all."

As the waitress moved away, Trista gazed out at the marina again. She mused, *So this is the place.* Her thoughts drifted back to another time, another life.

* * *

Holding the phone to her ear, she muttered, "Come on. Pick up. Pick up!"
He never took her calls. It was so frustrating. Why couldn't he just—

"Hello?" It was a miracle! A true miracle.

Trista tried to calm her voice. "Have you decided to change your
plans? I've been watching the weather report and I'm worried."

The voice on the other end just laughed. "No, we've come here to
have a good time. We're not going to let a little storm stop us."

She couldn't keep the tears back any longer. She sobbed, "Please
don't. Please wait a few days for this to pass—"

"You're being ridiculous. I just spoke with the charter boat captain,
and he assured me that there is no reason to worry. This is a big boat. It
can handle the waves."

Trista was now sobbing uncontrollably, unable to speak.

After a second, he became impatient. "Gotta go. We're boarding now.
I promise. We'll see you in a couple of days." Then he hung up.

She tried calling back. His phone was off.

She continued to sob. Unfortunately, this would end up like most of his
promises, empty and unfulfilled.

*   *   *

Startled, Trista jumped at the waitress's voice. "Are you OK?"

She hadn't realized it, but tears were running down her face. She
wiped with both hands trying desperately to dry her cheeks. "I'm fine. I'm
fine. Just an old memory."

Emma stood at the end of the table with the entrée. She slid it in front
of Trista and said quietly, "OK, but if you need anything, just let me
know."

The corners of Trista's mouth curled up weakly but failed to disguise her sad eyes. "Thanks, but I'm OK."

The waitress lingered a second longer than she might normally. "It's a man, isn't it?"

Trista nodded with the same sad smile. That was only partly true, but there was no need to go into the details.

"Well, they're all a sorry lot. Not one of them is worth the tears you shed. Just tell yourself that you deserve better."

Smiling through the tears, Trista asked, "Does that really work?"

"I keep trying it. I figure it's got to work one of these days." She laughed and Trista laughed with her.

"That's better." Emma smiled, turned, and left Trista to her meal.

Trista's appetite was gone. She spent several minutes pushing food around on her plate. When Emma returned, she looked at the mostly untouched meal and asked if the food was OK.

Trista laid her fork down and commented, "The food's fine. I've just lost my appetite, but you might be able to help me with something. How do I go about chartering a boat?"

The waitress smiled. "That's an easy one." She pointed across the way to a small building. "Just go to the marina office and ask for Cap. He can give you contact information for all the charters that run out of the marina."

Trista smiled. "Thanks"

The waitress added, "I'd do it soon though. Most charters will stop going out the closer the storm gets."

This was the bad news that Trista'd already suspected. She thanked the waitress and asked for the bill. Emma cleaned up the plates and left the check.

Leaving cash on the table to cover the bill and tip, Trista walked out of the restaurant and headed for the marina.

Chapter 6

Duck sat on the deck of the *Second Chance*, gazing out at the line of boats moored at the marina. She was an older twenty-four-foot sport-fishing boat with a walk-around cabin and dual 1300 outboard motors. The previous owner thought she looked good sitting at the dock behind his big waterfront home. One nasty divorce later, the boat, dock, and house were all sold. Cap knew the guy wanted to unload it quickly, so he was able to work out a great deal for Duck's mother. When she bought it, she'd hoped that Duck would run small charters on the Currituck Sound. But this was as far as Duck had ever taken her, tied up to the dock. Cap let him moor it just past the boat slips and didn't charge him a cent. When Duck was nine, his father passed away. It was devastating, but Cap stepped in to help the poor, struggling family. Off and on, he'd been helping them ever since.

As the boat rocked gently to the lullaby of the waves, Duck was taken back to the old rocking chair, now long gone from the deck at home. It was just after his father's funeral. They were receiving friends at their home. Duck was wrestling unsuccessfully with the loss and just wanted to be alone. Uncomfortable in a dress shirt and tie, he rocked on the deck as the waves ebbed and flowed just beyond as if nothing had changed.

The screened windows were open, and Duck could hear the well-wishers as they came and went. It was late in the day, and Cap and his son, Dean, were the only ones still there. His mother had successfully held things together during the funeral and in the hours following, but now she broke down. She sobbed uncontrollably, and he could hear Cap trying to console her. At one point, his mother sobbed, "I don't know how we're going to pay the bills or even put food on the table."

Cap's reply was calm and reassuring. "I'm sure that y'all will be OK." He paused for a moment. "You know, I could use some help around the marina. Why don't you have Duck stop by each day after school? I'm sure we can work something out."

That was the moment that Duck became the "man" of the family. That was the day he took the weight of the world on his shoulders. It was years before Duck realized that Cap had him work on his homework more than he had him help around the marina, yet Cap sent money to his mother each week for his "work." It was also years before he realized that Cap was paying way too much for the few hours of work he put in there. Cap was a good man. He kept Duck's family afloat without sinking their dignity. He became Duck's second father, teaching him about work and about life.

These were lessons taught through little moments, not by lecture. Duck was older before he understood the depth of these simple acts. One that he remembered fondly was a monthly chore that may have taken thirty minutes at most. Old man Simmons lived in a small, dilapidated houseboat that, for years, was moored where the *Second Chance* now sat. The boat's paint was peeling and was a chalky, dingy white. Oddly cut scraps of gray, weathered plywood were nailed in place on the deck to cover weakened, rotted areas. Duck only occasionally glimpsed inside the living area on those times that Cap would send him to make deliveries. The inside of the boathouse was smaller than his bedroom and darkly lit. On more than one occasion, Duck overheard other boat owners complaining to Cap about the "eyesore" at the end of the dock. Cap would listen patiently and thank them, but the boat remained moored there.

From what Duck could piece together from bits of adults' conversations, old man Simmons had been a good friend of Cap's father. While serving in the army, he caught shards of shrapnel in his skull and was never right after that. Sometimes Duck would see him standing on the deck of his boat arguing with the air or sitting on the stern, having a conversation with the seagulls.

Every month, around the twentieth, Cap would hand Duck cash and a list to take to the café. The cook would go back in the kitchen, throw some things together, and send him off with a bag full of food to deliver to old man Simmons. After the first few times, Cap no longer had to remind him of his lines. Duck would carry the bag onto the boat and knock on the door. Each time when the old man would answer, Duck would say, "Here's the food you ordered." The old man would stare blankly for a moment, blinking, as if trying to recover something lost. Then he would argue that he knew nothing about it and never ordered it. Duck would just smile and say, as instructed, "I can't take it back. You've already paid for it." At that point, the old man would scratch his head, mumble some indiscernible comments about forgetfulness and blessings, and then take the bag.

When Duck was young, he never quite understood this strange game, but then he didn't need to. Bag delivered, he was off to more important and interesting things. As he grew older, he became aware that old man Simmons lived on a very meager pension check that came in on the first of the month. Although Cap never said, Duck was certain that the old man never ordered the food or even paid for it. Cap, out of the goodness of his heart, sent the old man canned goods, meat, and fresh produce near the end of each month, somehow knowing that there was always more month than money. While some lessons are best learned with your head, these were lessons that Duck learned by heart.

Duck smiled at this recollection from his boyhood. He grew up wanting to be just like Cap. Maybe he was at one time, but Duck wasn't sure what kind of man he was now. Just as he did in the days following his father's death, he still carried the weight of the world on his shoulders. He would never say it and would never show it in his "I don't give a flip attitude," but it was there in the depths of his soul. Sissy probably knew. Without a doubt, Cap knew and was patiently waiting for Duck to free himself of the heavy shackles that held him submersed in torment. Sissy was right. Cap kept him on out of the goodness of his heart. The least that Duck could do is show up. He looked at his watch, 11:55. Duck stood, jumped onto the dock, and hands in pockets, wandered toward the marina office.

Looking up, he saw Trista crossing from the restaurant toward the marina. He sped up so that they reached the door at the same time. Duck opened the door and stepped back motioning for Trista to go first as he commented, "This is a real treat. I get to open the door for you twice today." He grinned.

Trista did not. She said, "Thanks," with no tinge of thankfulness as she stepped through the door.

Duck watched as she walked past, no smile, no other acknowledgment. His grin faded as he stepped in closing the door behind him.

Duck heard Cap's familiar voice before he was even in the door. "Be with you in a second young lady." As he stepped in and shut the door, Cap called out, "Duck, great. You're here. Can you help the young lady while Beau and me talk?"

Duck grimaced, if he'd known that Beau was inside, he wouldn't have come in. "Sure, be glad to." At least he had something to engage him away from Beau.

Trista turned toward Duck. "You work here?"

Duck nodded. His eyes darted from Trista over to Cap and Beau, who were in a low but agitated conversation, and back again. "What can I get for you?"

With a pained expression on her face, Trista hesitated. "I was told to ask for Cap."

Duck pointed over toward the escalating argument. "That's him, the older guy."

Trista glanced over. The older man was balding with a thinning, white fringe of raggedly cut hair running just below the shiny spot on the top of his head. He compensated for the lack of hair on top with a full, somewhat rough, white beard. His skin was dark and creased, almost like leather. Trista suspected that this was a man who had spent years in the sun and wind. He was shorter and slighter than the other man. Beau was a tall, solid man. His short-cropped, salt-and-pepper hair extended down his angular jawline, blending into a two-day stubble of a beard. His shoulders were broad and muscular, not like a weightlifter. He had the solid look of someone who was used to hard physical labor. Although their difference of opinion was quiet, Trista could tell that it was heated, and the volume was beginning to rise.

Duck interjected, drawing Trista's attention. "I've worked at the marina most of my life. I can probably help you."

Concerned that Cap's discussion wasn't going to end soon, Trista sighed and said flatly, "I'm looking for a charter boat."

Duck grinned. "I can help with that. We have a board over here where all the charters put up their contact information." He motioned her toward a corkboard mounted on the wall. As she moved toward the board, the argument at the other end of the room erupted.

Beau's voice hammered out each word. "This is ridiculous! You make a big deal about my late slip fee, but you let Ducky Boy tie up for free! You'll get your money!" He turned to storm out but heard Duck explaining to Trista about the information on the board.

Trying to ignore the escalating argument, Duck commented, "Most of the charters at this marina specialize in sound side fishing—"

Stepping between Duck and Trista, Beau extended his right hand and in a booming voice announced, "The name's Beau. I'm captain of the Blue Water Charters." As he spoke, he pounded the thick index finger of his left hand into a large Blue Water advertisement on the board. He was striking it so hard that the board shook, and Trista thought that it might fall. She hesitated and then reluctantly shook his hand.

Beau started up again, motioning toward Duck, "What rubber ducky here won't tell you is that Blue Water is the best charter for miles around."

Trista glanced over at Duck. With head bent, eyes focused on the floor, and pursed lips, he looked like a small boy being chastised by his father.

Beau continued, "Are you looking to go out today or tomorrow?"

Shifting her gaze back to Beau, Trista shook her head. "I'm looking for a charter for Thursday."

"Thursday?" Beau burst out laughing. "Have you been watching the weather on TV, Missy? This place is probably going to be hanging on for dear life come Thursday. If you'd like to change your plans to Monday, I think we could work something out."

Trista shook her head. "I think I'll call around to see if I can find someone for Thursday."

Chuckling, Beau replied, "OK, suit yourself, but you're not going to find anybody. Give me a call if you change your mind."

Beau pushed past Duck, knocking him off balance. He continued laughing as he stepped through the door into the bright sunlight.

Duck looked exhausted. His shoulders slumped, and the smile was gone. He quietly invited Trista to call any of the numbers on the board and then walked off, leaving her standing alone. She watched as he disappeared into a storeroom. She wondered why Beau had such animosity toward Duck. Why did Duck just take it without a word? Despite her disdain for Duck's apparent irresponsibility, she felt sorry for him. After a moment, she pulled out her phone and took photos of the flyers and cards on the board.

With the contact information stored in her phone, Trista left. At the door, she glanced back to find Duck absorbed in the task of restocking the refrigerated drink display case.

Chapter 7

Duck finished stocking the drinks and began returning misplaced snack, fishing, and boating items to their proper places on shelves and wall displays. Cap watched, knowing the shadowy figures and the ghastly scene playing out in Duck's silence.

"It's not your fault, you know." Cap waited for a response.

None came.

"Hey, Duck!"

Duck turned slowly, a pained look on his face.

"I said, you know it's not your fault."

They'd had this conversation before, and it always ended the same. Duck gave the old man a sarcastic smile and turned back to his quiet, tortured thoughts.

Ignoring Duck's feigned disinterest, Cap started up again. "Pretend all you want. I know that you can hear me. Someday you've got to stop beating yourself up over something that you couldn't control."

As usual, Duck ignored the comment. After a brief silent moment, Duck spoke without looking up. "You want me to open up that new box of lures and put them out?"

Cap had practically raised Duck and couldn't stand to see him do this to himself. He sighed, "Sure," as he stepped out the door for some fresh air.

Chapter 8

Knowing that Duck was at the marina made Trista feel more comfortable sitting out on her cottage deck. A tall glass of iced tea and cell phone in hand, she settled into a deck chair and began optimistically calling through the list of charters from the marina's board. An hour later, she deleted the last of the charter contacts and tossed the phone onto the table beside the empty glass. Tears welled up in her eyes and ran down her cheeks. She'd even called marinas farther south. Call after call, the voice on the other end said, "No," without hesitation.

What was she going to do? She *had* to go out on Thursday. Other days wouldn't work. She realized that she sounded like a crazy woman as she cried and pleaded in desperation during the last few calls. They didn't understand and they wouldn't. How could they? Trista hoped for their sake that they would never have to.

She watched as the waves rushed in and washed out in rhythmic motion, sand and shells deposited for an instant only to be carried out again. She marveled at how the shore was in constant change through a process that, ironically, had been unchanged since the start of time. Wasn't one day just the same as the next? Was she being unrealistic? Should she change her plans and go out earlier in the week? There were times in the past when she had been accused of having unrealistic expectations. He always accused her of being too serious. He treated life as just one big "whoops I'm sorry – are we good now?" Tears ran steadily down her face as she considered how everything to him, even their marriage, was a "whoops." She could still see the whole scene as if it were only yesterday.

*　　*　　*

Trista had been so excited. It was their tenth anniversary and she wanted it to be special. She asked him earlier in the week what he wanted to do to celebrate, and he was noncommittal, as usual.

With his attention fixed on the TV, he called out over his shoulder, "I don't know. I'm good with whatever you want to do." He really wasn't much for details. "Why don't you surprise me."

That was all the invitation that Trista needed. Immediately, ideas took on lives of their own. Maybe they would go to dinner at an upscale restaurant and take in a show. Maybe they would go on a sunset hot air balloon ride with a private landing site dinner. Perhaps they would rent a condo at the beach for the evening and then watch the sunrise over the ocean in the morning.

Each idea sounded grand, but in the end, Trista wanted something intimate, something that would be just theirs. She wanted to give him a special evening as part of a special gift. She decided to prepare a candlelight meal at home followed by an evening of intimacy. She loved cooking, and this would be her chance to give from the heart.

Days before the big event, she poured over recipes looking for just the right ones. She spent hours shopping for the freshest and the best ingredients for the meal. It had to be perfect.

She also went clothes shopping. She was looking for a sexy new dress. She didn't want just the meal to be special. She wanted to be special. She wanted to be wanted with the same type of electricity that ran hot when they first met. She went from store to store to find the right dress, one that revealed just enough to let the imagination do the rest. Finally, she found it. She put on a sultry, I want you, look as she slowly turned in front of the three-way mirror. She beamed with satisfaction. This was it.

Next, she went on the hunt for killer lingerie. She didn't want anything cheap or tawdry. She was looking for something that said nice girl gone naughty. After searching through several stores, she found a little number that caressed her curves. It covered, but the sheer material revealed enough to tease and tantalize.

Trista set out to make the table setting exceptional. Hours of shopping yielded strikingly beautiful new china and silverware and a gorgeous linen set for the table.

On the morning of their anniversary, she prepared to go to work as usual and acted as if it were just another day. He was preoccupied as usual, and she provided most of the morning chatter. "What time do you expect to be home tonight?"

"What?" He seemed a bit lost in the morning news broadcast. Some football player had been arrested for shooting two men outside a nightclub. "Oh, 6:30 like always."

Trista said rather nonchalantly, "OK. Well, don't be late. I'll have dinner ready."

"Sounds good," he said blankly, still engrossed in the news.

He normally left for work first. She kissed him goodbye and waited a safe period before she shed her suit and slipped into some comfortable clothes. She had secretly taken the day off from work so that she could prepare her surprise.

She spent the day cutting, preparing, and cooking. She ironed the new linens and set a romantic table with tall candles, freshly cut flowers, and quiet mood music in the background.

At about 5:30, with the meal well in hand, she showered, slipped on her new dress, freshened her makeup, added a touch of perfume and went downstairs to surprise him.

At first, she thought that he was just running a little late, but at 7:00 she called his cell. There was no answer. She began to worry. Was he OK? Could he have been in an accident? A quiet panic began to build.

She did the best she could to keep the food warm, but by 7:30 it wasn't the same meal. She continued to call without any luck. By 8:00, she was pacing and in tears, sure that he was in an emergency room somewhere.

At 8:15 when he pulled into the driveway, she felt like someone who'd been carried under by strong currents, finally breaking the surface and gasping in sweet air. She ran to the door to greet him.

As he opened the door, she threw her arms around his neck and sobbed in relief, "I thought... you... were dead." She could hardly get the words out.

He chuckled, "Having a few drinks with your boss might be unpleasant, but it won't kill you."

She pulled back in disbelief.

He looked at her. "Wow, you look great." Then he glanced through the doorway into the dining room. "Hey what's the special..." His voice trailed off as he realized the answer to his own question. He saw the storm raging in her eyes. "Honey, I'm sorry. If you'd just given me a heads up this morning—"

"Heads up? It's our anniversary and you need a heads up?" It was just like him. Everything was always her fault. He forgets their anniversary, and it's her fault.

His voice was consoling. "Come on, baby. We can still celebrate. The food smells wonderful and," he swept his hand toward the dining room, "you've gone to all this trouble."

She spun around, her heels clattering angrily on the hardwood floor as she strode away.

He called after her, "Come on, Trista. Don't do this. It's just another day. You always build things up to the point that they can never meet your expectations." He waved toward the dining room again. "Look at this. It's over the top!"

"Just another day? Our anniversary?" Trista's storm blew up. She screamed over her shoulder, "I'm going to bed. Don't bother to come upstairs!"

He looked up at the ceiling as his shoulders sagged.

*   *   *

"Just another day," she muttered. Trista slumped into the chair, exhausted. No, this wasn't about him. Who cared what he'd think? She was going to do what she knew she needed to do. It wasn't just another day. She would pray for a miracle and continue to look for a charter for Thursday. The plan wouldn't change.

Chapter 9

Long shadows of the cottages crept out across the beach until they floated on the constantly moving water. With each new wave, the peaks of the shadows danced and rippled on the water. The darkness of night was washing in quickly and so too was the tide. Trista stood and stretched. She had watched for hours as the water receded, shrinking into the ocean. Now it was slowly swallowing up the beach on its way back in.

Once inside the cottage, she turned on the TV and searched for the weather report. When the image of the spinning storm came on the screen, she felt the tears begin. It was huge, and nearly all the computer models showed it cutting straight through the Outer Banks.

She turned up the sound. "… sustained winds of one hundred and thirteen miles per hour. The National Hurricane Center has upgraded the storm to Category 3 status. The models haven't changed much over the past twenty-four hours. As you can see from the graphic, most models have Renee making landfall on the Outer Banks sometime early Thursday, traveling over Virginia, and then being pushed out to sea on Friday by this plunging front of cold air from Canada."

Trista flopped into one of the overstuffed chairs as if she'd sustained a blow to the midsection.

The diminutive weatherman continued, "There is one model, however…" He pointed to a line that brought the storm offshore and then headed northeast. "… that predicts the cold front will arrive earlier on Wednesday and push Renee out to sea just off the coast of North Carolina. This would be the best-case scenario; however, it is a long shot at this point."

Trista brightened. Maybe there was a chance. Suddenly, a scraping, banging noise from the seaside door startled her. She turned down the volume of the TV and listened. Again, she heard the banging. She rose and peered out the window. There was nothing. As she opened the door to step onto the deck, it swung open, and something brushed past her. Startled, she spun around to see Fetch flop onto the floor, exhausted from the effort of pushing his way through.

Her hand on her chest, she heaved a deep sigh of relief. "Dog, you gave me a heart attack." Fetch didn't move, evidently unconcerned. Trista swung the door open and called, "Here, Fetch."

The old dog lay, forepaws splayed out in front of him, head between them on the floor. His eyes moved in Trista's direction, but the rest of him was motionless.

"Come on, boy." Trista slapped her hands on her thighs. Fetch remained unresponsive.

Trista stood for a moment at a loss for another plan. She decided to help Fetch along. She stepped over to the prone dog and grabbed his collar, pulling up as she encouraged him, "Come on, boy. Let's go home." It was at that point that she realized that Fetch weighed almost as much as she did. She pulled, but the dog didn't budge.

She sighed in frustration. There had to be a way to get the dog back where he belonged. Food! She rummaged through the refrigerator and found a plastic container of lunch meat that she'd brought with her. She held one slice just beyond Fetch's reach. Interested, the old dog sniffed and then slowly rose to his feet. He stepped forward and snatched the slice from her hand. Now she was making progress. She backed through the door, calling him as she moved. Fetch ambled along. This continued every few feet along the dark stretch of sand that separated the two cottages. As she backed up the steps leading to the deck of the neighboring cottage, a voice startled her.

"Was that scoundrel begging for food at your door? I'm so sorry."

Trista jumped, her head jerking in the direction of the voice. In the dark, she could just make out the silhouette of a woman sitting in one of the chairs on the deck.

"Sorry, I didn't mean to startle you. I thought you saw me sitting here."

Trista exhaled and caught her breath, shaking her head. "No, I was focused on trying to get Fetch back over here. He pushed into my cottage and collapsed on the floor. Food was the only thing that would get him moving."

"Yeah, food is about the only thing that motivates him." Sissy paused. "Wait, did you call him Fetch?"

Trista looked confused. "Yeah, that's his name, isn't it?"

Sissy hesitated. "Sure, but how'd you know that?"

Trista exhaled with relief. "Oh, I'm sorry. Your boyfriend helped me get my door unstuck this morning. Fetch was with him."

Sissy's face revealed that she was lost. "My... boyfriend?"

Trista was still feeling like the two women were having entirely different conversations. "Yeah, Duck saw me struggling with the door and—"

Sissy broke out into uncontrollable laughter, interrupting Trista in mid-sentence and leaving her, mouth wide open, looking puzzled.

Between gasps of laughter, Sissy managed, "Duck's not... my boyfriend... He's my... brother."

Trista's cheeks grew flushed with embarrassment. She hoped that the dark hid the color rising in her face. "Sorry, I just thought," she stammered. "Well, I just… sorry." She wasn't making things any easier for herself. "I'm so embarrassed."

By this point, Sissy had regained her composure. "That's silly. Don't be. I probably would have made the same assumption."

"Well, I'm glad I was able to get Fetch back home 'cause I'm out of lunch meat." Trista smiled and held up the empty container. She started down the stairs toward the beach.

Sissy called out. "Hold on. Didn't I wait on you at the restaurant today?"

Trista stopped and turned, nodding. "Yeah, you did."

"Yep, I remember. You had the stuffed flounder, suffered from boyfriend-loss-of-appetite, and wanted information on charters. Was Cap able to help you?"

The full moon hung low over the sea casting a silvery light along the beach. Trista looked toward it as tears welled up in her eyes and ran down her cheeks. The moonlight sparkled in streams down her face. She fought to talk through the tears. "No, I talked to Duck—"

"Duck! What did that fool do?" Sissy's voice was sharp.

"No, it's not Duck. Actually, he was very helpful." The tears continued to stream down her face.

Sissy's voice became calm and consoling as she stood. "You know what? I think you could use a drink and someone to listen. Have a seat and I'll get you something to drink."

Trista shook her head, but her tears wouldn't stop. "No, I really should be going." She turned only to find that Fetch had flopped onto one of the steps below her making it impossible for her to leave.

As she stared at the dog below her, Sissy said, "See, even Fetch wants you to stay. Come on. I'm here all by myself, and it would be great to have someone to talk to."

Trista sighed with resignation. "Well, maybe just a while." She wiped at her tears as she climbed the steps onto the deck.

"You probably don't remember, but I'm Emma."

Trista nodded. "I remember. I'm good with names. I'm Trista."

"Well, it's good to meet you Trista." Sissy motioned to a chair. "Have a seat and I'll get you something. What would you like, soda, beer, wine?"

Trista thought for a moment. "I'm not sure. I don't drink much, but I could probably use something stronger than soda tonight." The truth was that Trista hadn't touched alcohol in years.

Sissy nodded knowingly. "I've got just the thing. It's a nice Moscato. I think you'll like it." She disappeared into the cottage and reappeared a few minutes later with a bottle and two wine glasses. Pouring one, she offered it to Trista and coaxed, "Try this. It's smooth."

Trista sipped the wine. It was sweet with just a bit of a bite. She took another sip and smiled. "It's good."

Sissy grinned. Pouring herself a glass, she sat down next to Trista. "So, if Duck didn't upset you, what's working on you so hard? Is it the boyfriend?"

Trista took another sip of the wine and shook her head. "No, that's really just a distant memory." Trista took another long sip from her glass and looked out at the moon. "Duck helped me with the contact information for charters. I spent all afternoon calling the numbers and can't get anyone to take me out."

Sissy looked baffled. "No one?" She paused. "That's hard to believe. They can't all be booked up."

Trista shook her head. "Not booked up. Just not going out… on Thursday." She glanced over at Sissy. "The storm's the problem."

Sissy still didn't understand. "Couldn't you get someone for Monday or Tuesday?"

Trista looked back toward the beach. "It has to be Thursday."

Sissy blurted out, "Why?"

Trista knew that no one would understand. She sighed, "It's hard to explain, but it's important." She was now looking straight into Sissy's eyes with an expression that carried sorrow or maybe despair mixed with the desperate determination of a rock climber dangling between the rocky ledge above and certain death below.

Sissy nodded slowly. "Well, I'm not sure that you'll get anyone willing to risk their boat and their life out in that storm, but I'd suggest talking to Jimbo at the café. He knows just about everybody around here. If anyone can make a connection for you, he can."

Trista's eyes were filling with tears again. She quietly said, "Thank you. I'll try that."

The two women sat in heavy silence for the next few minutes. Hoping to break the uncomfortable silence, Trista asked, "So, do you live here in the cottage, or does your brother?"

Sissy looked over with a crooked smile. "We both live here." She saw the surprise on Trista's face and continued. "Mom left the cottage to both of us when she passed. It's been a real financial struggle the past few years, so here we are. At least we have a roof over our heads."

Trista nodded as she looked out at the moon that was now hovering over the steady waves breaking along the beach. She was feeling warm and relaxed as the wine washed over her like the gentle waves on the shore. Feeling a bit loose, she explored more than she might normally. "How does Duck's girlfriend feel about him living with his sister?"

Sissy smiled. "Duck doesn't have a girlfriend. He's never been married and hasn't been in a relationship in years."

Trista considered the answer for a few seconds. "I know that he's rough around the edges, but don't you think it's odd that he's so unattached?" She paused. "I mean he is a good-looking man." The wine had loosened her up.

Sissy gave a deep sigh and shrugged. "It's not that women haven't been interested. He's had several chase him in the past, but he's never given them the time of day."

Trista gave her a questioning look. "Really?"

Sissy continued, "It's complicated. On the outside, he seems irresponsible and immature. That's what he wants you to see so that you don't get too close to what's beneath the veneer. Duck wasn't always the slap-happy fool that you see. Our father passed away when he was very young." She took a sip of wine and continued. "You know, I'm older, but I think it was Duck that held us together during those dark days... and after."

Trista detected a slight quiver in Sissy's voice. She gave her a moment to gain composure and then asked the obvious. "What changed Duck?"

Sissy sniffled and dabbed at the corners of her eyes. "I'm sorry. It's hard for me to talk about it because it breaks my heart to see him like this. Duck refuses to talk about it." She took a deep breath and exhaled. "There was an accident. Several people died. One of them was his best friend in high school. A lot of people around here blame Duck." She sobbed as she choked out the next sentence. "The worst... part is... he blames himself." Sissy was now sobbing uncontrollably.

Trista reached over and placed her hand reassuringly on Sissy's arm, allowing her to work through her sorrow quietly.

Slowly, Sissy regained composure. Wiping away the last of the tears, she sniffled, "I'm sorry. I said I'd help you with your problems, and now here we are running a counseling session for me. I'm sure that Duck and I seem like a hot mess." She smiled weakly.

Trista watched the rhythmic wash of the waves on the shore. Then sadly she commented, as if to the ocean, "No, I understand completely."

Sissy suspected that she really couldn't understand but appreciated the comment.

After an awkward, quiet moment, Trista broke the silence. "I need to be getting back. Thanks for the wine. It was really good. And thanks for listening." She stood.

Sissy offered, "Are you sure you wouldn't like a second glass?"

Trista declined, indicating that she was tired. She paused at the top of the stairs, looking down. It took Sissy a second to realize why she didn't move. She called out, "Fetch, come." The old dog rose slowly, ambled past Trista, and slumped onto the deck at Sissy's feet. She ran her bare foot along the retriever's back and cooed, "Good dog."

Trista waved and stepped down to the beach below. As she walked, she called back, "Thanks again for the drink and conversation."

"Anytime, I can always use some female company after a day of Duck."

They both laughed as Trista made her way across the sand. As she walked, she felt sorry for Sissy. She seemed to be carrying a heavy burden. If anything, Trista understood what that was like. In very different ways, they were both dealing with loss. She looked back as she opened the door of her cottage. In the dark, she could make out Sissy's silhouette sitting motionless on the deck.

Chapter 10

Sissy glanced at her watch. It was half past midnight and no Duck. It was time to go find him. She'd worked out a system with Jimbo to cut Duck off at twelve. For weeks after, Duck had fumed and complained to anyone who would listen that he was an adult and could make his own decisions about when to stop drinking. Most people didn't listen, and after a while, he just came to accept it. He was usually home by 12:30, but now and then she had to go find him. She had a good idea where he would be.

Sissy drove the short distance to the café and swung into the gravel lot. As she stepped into the restaurant that had the feel of a bar at night, Jimbo called out, "He left at midnight." To even the casual observer, it was obvious that this was a routine that both were very familiar with.

Sissy nodded and called back, "Thanks, Jimbo," as she headed out the door. She crossed the parking lot, walking toward the boat slips. The gravel crunched under her feet in the quiet night. When she reached the *Second Chance*, she called out, "Duck?" There was no answer. She tried a second time with the same result. She boarded the boat and peered through the open cabin door. In the dark, she could barely make out the jumble of scuba gear, fishing rods, tackle boxes, and floatation devices. In the middle of the dark tangle, she could see two feet. It wasn't uncommon for Duck to crash on the boat to sleep one off.

Sissy smacked one foot with her hand. "Duck, wake up. Time to go home." She waited, but there was no response. She tried again, but Duck was motionless. He could easily have been mistaken for dead if not for the rattling snore that came from the dark recesses of the cabin. Sissy pulled a cold bottle of water from the tiny cooler sitting by the door, opened it, and tossed the water in the general direction of the snoring. There was immediate thrashing and coughing as Duck sat up, stunned by the cold liquid.

"Are you crazy? You almost drowned me," he shouted between coughs.

Sissy stood in the doorway, hands on her hips, waiting for the coughing to end. Once Then, she barked, "Come on. Let's go." She'd been through this too many times in the past to beat around the bush.

Duck stood unsteadily, wiped his wet face with his shirt, and mumbled, "All you had to do was ask."

Sissy ignored the comment.

Duck weaved and stumbled on the gently rocking deck. Sissy struggled to help him from the boat without being thrown into the water. Finally, she pulled Duck onto the steadier planks of the dock and exhaled with relief and exhaustion. As the two crossed the parking lot, Duck asked, "What about my vehicle?"

Sissy said, "Leave it. We'll get it in the morning."

Duck stopped, indignant. "What if someone steals it?"

Sissy shouted over her shoulder as she continued to walk, "Get real, Duck. No one wants that piece of junk!"

Duck hesitated, shrugged, and then followed Sissy to her car.

Back at their home, Sissy helped her unsteady brother up the steps and into the small cottage. As soon as he was in, Duck crashed face down on the sofa. In disgust, Sissy said, "Good night, Duck." She walked back toward her bedroom, exhausted from the effort required just to get Duck home. Let him sleep wherever. At least she knew he was safe. Before closing her bedroom blinds, she looked across the way to the brightly lit windows of Trista's cottage.

Chapter 11

Trista sat, enveloped in one of the overstuffed chairs in her cottage, weary and a bit woozy from the wine. She wasn't sure if the exhaustion was from dealing with her own problems or from sharing in Sissy's distress. Either way, she welcomed the opportunity to sleep. She rose and turned out the lights as she climbed the stairs to her bedroom. She changed and collapsed into bed hoping that she would sleep through the night. Sleep had been a stranger for the past few years, but in more recent months it had become impossible because of the fitful dreams. They weren't really nightmares, just unsettling. The dreams had been the motivation for this trip. The real nightmare was the churning storm out in the Atlantic and its possible effect on her plans. Trista's memories ebbed and flowed like the waves just outside her window. With the same mesmerizing rhythm, they drifted her off to sleep. But restful slumber would not last.

Trista jerked awake, breathing heavily. She checked the clock on the nightstand. The lighted display read 4:14. She sat up willing herself to breathe more slowly… inhale deeply… exhale slowly. Eventually, her breathing became steady. It was the dream. The one that had touched and troubled her for months. She felt that it was leading her on, calling to her, indicting her for her inattention to something important. She felt the heavy burden of guilt and was haunted by the compelling need for redemption.

She knew all too well that there would be no more sleep tonight. Wearily she moved to the kitchen and started up a fresh pot of coffee. Hot, steaming cup in hand, she stepped out onto the deck. The moon, now high overhead, was a writhing splash of light on the ever-moving water. She sat and listened to the lapping of the gentle waves. It was hard to believe that, in just days, this scene would be one of a thrashing, foaming creature that would crush houses in its watery jaws.

Trista was startled from the waves' hypnotic trance by motion near the shore. There in the night stood a dark figure. She hadn't noticed him at first because he had been motionless, but now he bent down, picked up some object from the wash, and in a sidearm motion tossed it back into the ocean. Out of the dark, loped the shadow of a large dog. It splashed into the surf next to the man who reached down and ruffled the dog's coat with one hand. It was Duck and Fetch. She watched as they slowly made their way down the beach and disappeared into the darkness.

Trista felt sad for the burden he must be carrying, but she just couldn't see him as Sissy had described him. From her experience with men, they were all the same, careless, immature, and irresponsible. Duck seemed no different than other men that she had known. As scene after scene of disappointment played out in the dark before her, the endless chain of sleepless nights weighed down her eyelids, slowly floating her into a deep sleep.

Chapter 12

Trista woke with a start, the bright sun well above the horizon. She blinked, looking around, lost for a moment. Eventually she stood and stretched, trying to shake off the stiffness from sleeping in the hard deck chair for hours. From a distance, she heard a voice call out, "Mornin' neighbor." She looked in the direction of the voice to find Sissy standing out on the neighboring cottage's deck. She raised what appeared to be a cup of coffee in salute. "Long night huh?"

Trista nodded.

"Well, if you'd like some coffee, I've got a pot on."

Trista smiled. "Thanks for the offer, but I need to get cleaned up and hit the road. I'm already behind schedule."

Sissy called back, "Where you headed?"

"Elizabeth City."

Sissy nodded. "Yeah, you've got a bit of driving to do. If you change your mind about the coffee, just come on over."

"Thanks." Trista waved as she started to push through the door only to find it stuck. She banged into the door to Sissy's amusement. Stepping back, she held up her hand to pause the laughter. She jiggled the door as she had seen Duck do the day before. Pushing with one hand and slapping with the other, she freed the door and swung it open. She turned toward Sissy with both hands pointing toward the door, palms up like one of those girls on the TV game shows displaying a prize. Sissy set down her mug and applauded with a mock look of approval. Trista waved again and stepped through the open door. She thought, *Sissy seems to be a genuinely nice person.*

In the shower, Trista let the warm water pour over her, trying to wash away the remnants of her stiffness. Once out, she toweled off and dressed quickly. She felt excitement and fear all in the same moment. This was something that she'd looked forward to for weeks, and yet she wasn't sure what she'd do or say. What if he didn't want to see her? She'd just have to take the chance. Trista gave herself one last glance in the mirror. The glint of her necklace caught her off guard. She paused, lightly touching the silver half-heart. This was important.

Outside in the car, she entered her destination in the GPS. As the crow flies, Elizabeth City would be a quick trip. Unfortunately, she wasn't a crow. She would have to drive south for miles to reach the Wright Memorial Bridge, only to turn north and drive miles again and then turn west toward Elizabeth City. That was the reality of traveling to and from the Outer Banks. The drive time would be just over an hour, but she had all day.

She drove south along Route 12 passing cottages and shrub brush, only occasionally catching a glimpse of the Currituck Sound to the right. The ocean-themed tourist shops that dotted the roadway and the cottages running off to both sides of her were witnesses to the presence of the sea and the sound, but she felt eerily detached from the water. She thought that it was funny that she could be so close and yet feel so far away.

As she swung onto Route 158, headed toward the bridge, she knew that it would take her the rest of the way. She was now on autopilot as the GPS fell silent. She turned on the car stereo, synced it with her phone, and then brought up one of her well-worn playlists. Settling in for a long drive, she allowed herself to get lost in the music.

The songs made the time pass quickly as she sang along with some and just listened to others. As she approached the town of Grandy, the first familiar chords of Chris Young's "Drowning" brought a sad smile at the certain knowledge that she was going to cry. The lyrics were quickly lost in a memory that she had revisited over and over.

*   *   *

They were planning her daughter's ninth birthday, and Trista was desperately trying to get some gift ideas. She asked Angie for suggestions and was surprised when the first hand-scrawled item on her daughter's list was to be baptized. They had been talking about it for a while. Trista wanted to be sure that she understood the significance of baptism. She seemed ready, so Trista was thrilled to see her request listed above the MP3 player, doll, and clothes.

They planned a mommy-daughter shopping trip to find just the right dress to wear to church on the day of the baptism. Trista thought it would also be nice to find a silver necklace with a cross pendant as a reminder of the big day. They headed out to the mall early one Saturday and spent all morning looking at dresses. They'd go through the racks, pull out an arm-full of dresses, and then take them back to the fitting room to give each one a twirl in front of the mirror. Store after store, this continued. Some were dismissed as soon as they were on. Others were considered as possible, but the search continued.

Trista and Angie took a break, and Trista treated her to lunch at one of her favorite restaurants. The waiters prepared the food tableside, and Angie was always fascinated with the theatrical preparation and the accompanying patter. Trista studied Angie's look of amazement and wondered how much longer her childlike joy in simple things would last. She'd tried to hide her tears as Angie twirled around in a few of the dresses that made her look so old. She was losing her baby.

After lunch, the search continued. With almost four hours of shopping behind them, they found it. The dress was perfect. It was a white dress made of layers of sheer, flowing material that moved gently as she walked.

Angie loved it. She spun in front of the mirror again and again. Trista loved it too. They bought the dress and headed off to a little silver shop in the mall to find the perfect necklace.

Angie's eyes lit up as she moved from one display case to the next. There were so many beautiful things to see. Trista let her look and dream and then tried to pull her back on task.

"Angie, the cross necklaces are over here."

Angie wandered over and spent some time studying each one. Trista asked the clerk to take a few out. Angie tried each one on, smiling as she modeled for the mirror. After a few minutes, Trista asked, "So, which one would you like?"

Angie looked down at the shining necklaces in the display case for a long moment and then looked up at her mother with wide eyes.

"Mommy, will you promise that you won't be mad?"

Surprised, Trista said hesitantly, "Of course not. Why would I be mad?"

"Because I don't want one of these necklaces. I want one over there," she said pointing to a display case on the other side of the store.

Trista promised not to be upset, but she was. She brought Angie here to get a special reminder of her baptism, not to buy just any old piece of jewelry. She tried hard not to show her disappointment. In her best soothing voice, she coaxed, "Well, why don't you show me the necklace that you want?"

The worried expression melted from Angie's face, and she jumped up and down as a bright smile took its place. Running over to the other display case, she pointed to a display. "This is the one I want. I think it's special, don't you?"

It wasn't one necklace. It was two. Trista could hardly breathe as she looked on in shame and joy at the shining necklaces in the case. Together they made the shape of a heart, each being a half. Engraved on one was "Always Together." On the other, "Never Apart." Then running across the two pieces was engraved,

Mother – Daughter

Sharing One Heart

The sign below the necklaces announced that names would be engraved on the reverse side as part of the purchase.

Trista's eyes filled with tears that escaped and streamed down her cheeks. Angie's smile melted, "What's wrong, Mommy? Did I upset you?"

Trista tried unsuccessfully to wipe the tears from her face. "No, no, sweetheart. You didn't upset me. I'm just touched that you would want to share this necklace with me."

*   *   *

Trista jerked back into the present as tires screeched and car horns blared. A pickup truck skidded past banging over the curb and onto the grass next to her. A car slammed to a stop just short of the driver's side door of her car as she sped through the intersection. She looked back in the rearview mirror to discover the traffic light was red behind her. It appeared that the other two vehicles were OK. She glanced back again to see both back on their original path and driving off. Shaken and embarrassed, she exhaled deeply and ran the fingers of her right hand over both moist cheeks until the streams of tears subsided.

She turned off the music. She didn't want a repeat of what almost happened back there. The music in her playlist always brought back memories. It was miles before she regained composure. She drove the rest of the way in silence.

Chapter 13

Duck stood in the sunlight outside the marina office, squinting against the bright sun. He felt like a boat that had run aground on sharp rocks and been pounded by heavy surf. Too much alcohol and too little sleep were a lethal combination. Unfortunately, they were also a frequent combination. Duck was just about to call it a day and try again tomorrow when Cap's voice called from behind him, "Mornin', Duck." Too late.

Cap walked past him and held the door open as he stepped through. Duck shook his head as he followed. At least it wasn't so insufferably bright inside. Duck went into the back room and pulled out cases of drinks. He toted them to the cooler, opened the glass door, and began restocking the bottles and cans. Cap was back in the small office, working on paperwork. Behind him, Duck heard the door swing open and then close. He turned to see a neatly groomed man who looked to be about his age. His hair was trimmed and brushed back stylishly. He wore a starched blue dress shirt open at the collar, sharply pressed khaki slacks, and polished black loafers. There was something familiar about him. As Duck studied him trying to sort it out, the man was returning the gaze with a similar expression of curiosity. Then a broad smile swept across his face. "Duck?" He spread his arms as if welcoming an old friend. "It's me… Dean." Duck's face brightened with recognition.

"Dean! Look at you all cleaned up. I almost didn't recognize you."

Dean smiled at the comment. He'd spent his entire high school career trying to win Duck's approval.

"What brings you all the way from D.C. to this little puddle?"

After high school, Dean cobbled together several small scholarships and went on to attend UNC–Charlotte. After graduation, he was accepted into law school at William and Mary. A prestigious law firm in D.C. that was always looking for top students from top law schools recruited him and brought him to northern Virginia. It was a long trip for a boy from a small school in a small community. He looked the part of the big-time, successful attorney.

Dean looked around the small shop. "Where's my old man?"

Duck motioned over his shoulder with his thumb, "In the back… paperwork."

"I thought that I'd drive down here and surprise him. See if I can convince him to come spend a few days with us until this storm passes."

Duck chuckled, "Good luck."

Dean smiled and nodded. "I know. I know. Hey, I've got to give it a try. I worry about him trying to ride out the storm by himself. You remember what it was like with Isabel. That house was like an island, water all around and underneath. If it had collapsed, there would have been no escape." Dean's face reflected his concern but then brightened. "Let me go back here and see the old man, and then maybe you and I can do some catching up. You know, driving down here I was thinking about the state swim meet of our senior year. That was epic." Dean nodded and grinned. He didn't notice Duck wince at his last comment.

Duck responded flatly, "Yeah, let's get together."

"Sounds good," Dean chirped as he moved toward the back office.

As Dean slipped out of sight through the doorway, Duck exhaled deeply, opened the drink cooler, grabbed a can of beer, and walked out the door into the sunlight. He needed to recover. He dragged himself down the dock as he popped the tab and slugged down the icy liquid. He hopped onto the *Second Chance* and sat down to finish the beer. Letting his thoughts stumble from his mouth, Duck mumbled, "State swim meet, yeah… epic." He studied a dead tree limb as it drifted by. As it did, his thoughts also drifted back to a time when he was on top of the world.

*   *   *

Duck loved it, the smell of the chlorine, the sounds of the crowd echoing off the walls, the rush of the competition. This was his high school senior year, his last state championship. He wanted to savor it. He tried to take it all in and trap it there so that it would be there for years to come.

Unfortunately, the rules would only allow him to compete in two individual events and two relays. He could probably win at all four strokes, but his best were 100 free and 100 breast, so that's where he was entered. As the women's 100 freestyle finals got underway and he prepared for the men's next, he heard a voice calling out, "Duck, Duck." He looked over to find Dean shouting and waving his hands. "Duck, new state record! I can feel it!" Duck smiled for just a moment, but quickly retreated within himself, focusing on the task at hand. The echoed cheering and shouting evaporated. Inside his head it was quiet and serene. He watched the women end and exit the water as if in slow motion.

As the participants in the men's 100 freestyle were called to the blocks, he looked to his left. Two lanes over was his best friend Brody. Brody looked up and caught Duck's eye. They nodded to each other, all business. There were two unfortunate facts about the finals. The first was that Brody's two best strokes were Duck's two best strokes, so they were swimming against each other in the free and the breast. The other unfortunate fact was that Brody had never beaten Duck in a competition. Although they were best of friends, that fact had become a sore point on more than one occasion.

"Swimmers take your marks… set…" Once the tone sounded, it was all about translating power into smooth, flawless execution – perfect entry,

perfect stroke form, perfect turn. For Duck, swimming was as effortless as breathing was for other people. In a matter of seconds, it was over. Turning toward the scoreboard, Duck emerged from the water, pulled off his goggles, and slapped the water with both hands as he saw his time, a new North Carolina high school record.

As he walked from the pool, Dean ran to him with a towel and slapped him on the back. "I told you! A new record! I could feel it!" Dean was the team manager and one of Duck's biggest boosters. He seemed to be even more excited than Duck. During the excitement, Duck looked over to the stands, his mother and sister were jumping up and down and screaming. He noticed Brody looking toward the door leading out of the pool where Brody's father and older brother, Beau, were leaving. Brody watched as they exited, never looking back. His shoulders slumped as he slowly walked toward the locker room. Duck looked back at the scoreboard. Brody had taken the silver medal, but there was no celebration. Duck felt his best friend's burden. Brody was always second best, never as good as his older brother, never as good as Duck, and always a disappointment to his father. Brody would never talk about it, but Duck saw him constantly trying to win his father's approval and constantly falling short.

As Duck and Dean walked toward the locker room with Dean still chattering excitedly about the new record, the swim coach for State stopped them. "Congratulations! That was a great race. You're a very talented young man. I hope you're still considering State."

Duck looked around uncomfortably. "Well, I haven't made a decision yet."

The coach smiled. "You know, you're a gifted swimmer. You should be pointing toward the Olympics. We've got a great program, and we can get you there."

"I'll think about it." Looking around, Duck said, "I've got to get ready for my next race."

Still smiling, the coach chuckled, "OK, I'll let you go. Just remember to keep us in mind."

As Duck and Dean entered the locker room, Dean said wistfully, "It must be nice to have every college coach chasing after you."

Duck exhaled, "Not really. I'm not interested in college."

Dean stopped, "Are you crazy? I'd kill for the opportunities that you have."

Draping the towel over his shoulders, Duck commented, "School's not my thing. I want to do something important. I want to make a difference." He was looking beyond Dean off somewhere into the future. "I want to help people."

*   *   *

Duck's thoughts were cut short by a voice calling his name. He looked down the dock to see Cap and Dean. Cap was calling out to him. He thought how in life's ironic twists and turns his wish had come true. Here he was at the marina helping people fuel their boats and find fishing gear and their favorite beverage… not exactly what he envisioned years ago.

As Dean and Cap reached the *Second Chance*, Dean looked the boat over enviously. "Nice boat. How does she handle?"

Duck shrugged with a hang-dog expression. The truth was that he didn't know.

Dean pressed on. "Come on. How fast—"

"She runs like a boat," Cap interjected. "Enough of this chit-chat." He motioned to Duck. "We're going for lunch at the café. Why don't you join us? I'm buying."

Duck hesitated.

Cap prodded, "Come on, Duck. Dean doesn't visit that often."

Offended, Dean shouted, "Hey, that was a cheap shot."

Cap laughed but stood expectantly watching Duck. Sighing, he set down his beer, stood, and joined the two men on the dock. Together they crossed the gravel lot to the restaurant.

As they entered the café, Cap called out to Jimbo, "Look what the cat dragged in."

Jimbo's puzzled expression evaporated as he shouted, "Dean!" He hurried out to greet them, wrapping Dean up in a smothering bear hug.

Dean slapped his back, "OK, Jimbo, don't crush me."

The big man released him and stepped back to look him over.

"Dean, you look the part of a big-city lawyer."

Dean beamed at the comment. Gesturing to the sign above the bar, he remarked, "Hey, Jimbo, what's with the name change? Last time I was here, this place was the *Catch of the Day*.

Duck jabbed, "Wow, it has been a long time since you've been here."

Dean frowned as he shot Duck a sharp look.

Jimbo's smile went from ear to ear. "I bought the place six years ago and changed the name right away."

Amazed, Dean asked, "So you're the owner now, not the bartender?"

Jimbo nodded smiling proudly, "Yep, owner, chief executive officer… and bartender."

All four men chuckled.

Dean was still curious about the name. "But why *The One That Got Away*? It's a bit long don't you think?"

Jimbo shook his head, "No, the best fishing stories are always about the one that got away. The fish are always bigger, the fight is always harder, and the heartbreak is always greater." Jimbo brought his hands together interlacing his fingers. "Truth and imagination get so tangled up that you can't separate them." Dropping his hands, he smiled. "It's perfect."

Realizing that he'd become a bit long-winded, Jimbo commented, "Well, guys, you're here to eat, not listen to me jabber. Have a seat. I'll get your drinks. What would you like?" Dean and Cap ordered water. Duck asked for beer.

"A little early in the day for beer, isn't it, Duck?" Sissy slid up from behind Jimbo. "Aren't you working?"

Cap held up his hand. "It's OK. We're celebrating Dean coming to visit."

Sissy had been so focused on Duck that she had missed Dean. "Dean! Decided to come visit the common folks, huh?"

Dean chuckled as the three men took their seats.

"I'll give you gentlemen a few minutes to look over the menu. I'll help Jimbo with your drinks." She glared briefly at Duck and then slipped away.

Dean turned to Cap, "I was telling Duck that, as I was driving down, I couldn't help but think about the state swim meet our senior year. The breaststroke final was epic." As Dean chattered on about the race, Duck got lost in his own memory of that day.

*   *   *

The breaststroke was the last individual final of the meet. This was Brody's best stroke, but even at that, he had not been able to beat Duck. Standing on the blocks, Duck looked down the line to Brody, who stared up at the high ceiling of the aquatic center and exhaled slowly as if wishing on some distant star. This was the last race of their high school career.

As the starting tone sounded, Duck settled into his rhythm, perfect entry, perfect stroke form, perfect turn. Nearing the end of the race, he stole a glance to both sides. He had a slight lead on Brody. There was no one else in contention. All it would take was perfection.

As Duck emerged from the water, he didn't look at the scoreboard. He knew the results. Instead, he looked up in the stands and found Brody's father and brother pumping their fists and screaming like they were crazy. Across the pool, Brody was slapping the water and roaring. Duck smiled.

*   *   *

Dean grabbed Duck's attention. "Duck… Duck, I watched every one of your races in high school and never saw you misjudge the touch at the end like you did that day."

At that moment Sissy showed up with the drinks.

Duck said casually, "Got water in my goggles. Couldn't see the wall."

As Sissy placed Duck's beer on the table, she gave him a long hard stare. The others didn't notice. He wasn't sure if it was because of the beer or because of his comment.

Just then a voice boomed from the direction of the door. "Well, well, well, I wondered who owned the Mercedes in the parking lot. It's long-lost Dean." Beau strode up to the table where the three were seated. "I heard you were a fancy lawyer now. I guess that's why you're sitting with the murderer." He directed his comment more toward Duck than Dean. Duck didn't look up. Instead, his head hung as he focused on the tabletop.

Cap spoke up. "Come on, Beau. Let's not do this now. We're just trying to eat lunch."

Beau bored a hole in Duck with his eyes. "Sure, let my brother's killer eat lunch."

Sissy put her hand on Beau's arm, "Come on Beau. Leave Duck—" Before she could finish, he shoved her backward, sending her stumbling into one of the tables. Silverware, condiment bottles, salt and pepper shakers clanged and crashed to the floor.

Duck would take any abuse Beau could dish out, but he wouldn't stand for anyone pushing his sister. He attempted to stand, but Beau anticipated and sent a fist crashing into his face. Half sitting, half standing, Duck was off balance, and the blow sent him sprawling to the floor. His chair went clattering in the other direction. As he attempted to stand, Beau grabbed his shirt with both hands and jerked him upright. Feeling his feet beneath him again, Duck drove his right hand up between Beau's arms, thrusting the heel of his hand toward Beau's face. Beau turned at the last moment and Duck's hand slammed into the side of Beau's nose and his left eye. He released his grip on Duck's shirt as he stumbled backward. Holding his face, Beau let out a string of profanity.

By this time, Jimbo had found his way between the two men. Cap and Dean joined him. Sissy was holding Duck. Beau considered rushing him, but Jimbo alone was bigger than Beau. The odds weren't in his favor, and he knew it.

"I don't know why everyone protects this piece of trash," he yelled, pointing at Duck. "I've lost my appetite." Beau strode off toward the door, shoving tables and chairs out of his path. Near the door, he wiped a stream of blood from just below his nose. Looking down at the red smear on his hand, he turned and shouted, "Next time you won't have your sister to protect you." He turned and stormed out.

Sissy looked at Duck's face. His jaw was red and swelling quickly. She dragged him back to the kitchen to put ice on it.

Cap looked over at Dean and exhaled trying to compose himself. "Beau's a lucky man."

Dean gave his dad a puzzled look. "Lucky?"

"Yeah, Duck may act like a whipped puppy, but there's a storm inside him that could tear anything apart, even Beau."

Chapter 14

The electronic voice of the GPS broke the silence, "In two-tenths of a mile turn left onto South Hughes Boulevard, Route 17." Trista knew from her earlier study of the map that she was nearing her destination. She made her turn and soon the GPS announced, "In two-tenths of a mile turn left onto Halstead Boulevard, Route 344." After making her second turn, she drove for about three miles before the GPS announced, "Approaching your destination on the left." Trista's heart raced as she saw the sign – United States Coast Guard, Base Elizabeth City, NC. The small sign was surrounded by two full-scale display airplanes, a helicopter, and a boat. Each bore the Coast Guard insignia. She turned her car into the entrance road not knowing exactly what to expect.

About thirty yards down the entrance road, she arrived at a small guard station. The uniformed young man searched briefly for a base sticker. Seeing none, he stopped her. She slid down the window as he stepped to the side of the car. "Military ID, ma'am?"

"Sorry, I don't have one. I'm trying to contact a person who was stationed here a while back. I'm hoping he's still here." She was counting on her lost and helpless look to make a difference. It didn't.

The guard was all business. "Did this person call ahead to arrange for a visitor's pass for you?"

Trista smiled. "That's just the problem. I don't know how to contact him. His name's Petty Officer Jason Mallory. Maybe you know him."

"No, ma'am. I don't know him. I'm sorry but you can't come on base without a prearranged pass."

Trista sat, unsure of what to do. "Isn't there some way to get in touch with him?"

The guard glanced up at the line of vehicles beginning to form behind Trista's car. "You could try calling the main number for the base. There is also a personnel locator page on the Coast Guard website."

Trista sat speechless. She hadn't anticipated this.

After a brief, silent moment, the guard spoke. "I'm sorry, ma'am. You can turn here to exit."

Stunned, Trista made a U-turn around the guard station and headed back out to the highway. This couldn't be how this trip ended.

Passing the display planes and helicopter on her way out, she turned and headed back toward the Outer Banks. She hadn't come all this way to give up so easily. She pulled into a small strip mall and parked. Fishing her cell phone from her purse, she called directory assistance. In a moment, she was listening to the recorded menu of options from the Coast Guard base's main number. None of them seemed to be exactly what she needed. As the menu cycled through again, she selected one that mentioned personnel. She became excited when the line picked up. Just as quickly, her heart dropped at the recording that asked her to leave a message. She couldn't wait for hours to get a response. She needed to speak to a live person now. She called back a second time. This time she chose a different menu item. Again, a different recorded voice invited her to leave a message. She called a third time only to get a similar response. Her eyes filled with tears. She hadn't expected to have this much difficulty making contact. As she wiped at the streams that now ran down her cheeks, her attention was drawn to one of the storefronts in the strip mall. Above the door was a sign that read AIR STATION DINER. A cardboard sign in the window declared, COAST GUARD DISCOUNT. It was lunchtime. Maybe someone inside would be able to help her.

Stepping inside, she stood for a second and scanned the room. Most of the tables in the small diner were empty. At one table, she noticed two uniformed young men. They appeared to be straight out of high school. She was uncomfortable but she was also desperate. Trista pushed herself toward the table, fixed a smile on her face, and interrupted the conversation. "Excuse me. Maybe you can help me." The two young men looked up in surprise. "I'm looking for a Coast Guardsman."

One of the men who had the good looks of a heartbreaker flashed a smile and extended his arms out, palms up. "You just found one, beautiful."

Trista blushed. She was almost old enough to be his mother. She was shocked at his response. She wouldn't admit it, but she was also flattered that he would call her beautiful. She stammered, trying to recover and finish. "No, no, I'm looking for someone who was stationed here a few years ago. His name is Jason Mallory."

The other young man had a thoughtful look on his face. "Can't place him, can you Jones?"

Jones was still smiling at Trista. "Don't know the guy, but I'm sure that I can do anything he could do… only better." His friend began chuckling.

Trista's smile turned to a sarcastic sneer. "Maybe you should ask your momma if you can play with the big girls. Thanks for the help."

The friend began cackling even louder as she spun around and headed out the door.

Jones called out to her, "Hey baby, don't leave me here brokenhearted." The door closed behind her.

She took a deep breath as she slid into her car. This trip was a bust. Now she needed to focus on the charter for Thursday. It had to happen.

Back on the road, she glanced at herself in the rearview mirror and wondered, *Did he really think I was beautiful?* She settled in for the long drive back, occasionally glancing at her reflection in the mirror.

Chapter 15

Sissy snatched a quart-sized zip lock bag and scooped crushed ice from the freezer into it. "Here," she commanded. "Hold this on your jaw."

"Agghh!" Duck winced as he gingerly placed the ice on the side of his face. Sissy grabbed his free arm and dragged him toward the kitchen door leading to the back of the café. Duck complained, "What are you doing?"

Sissy continued pulling on him as she snapped, "Get outside… now." Duck knew the tone. He didn't want to go but wasn't going to anger her more.

Outside, behind the restaurant, Sissy turned on him. "What was that in there?"

Duck looked puzzled. "I wasn't going to let Beau push you like that."

Sissy's volume rose. "That's not what I'm talking about."

Duck looked lost. "What then?"

"First, what are you doing drinking during the workday?"

Duck shrugged, "You heard Cap. It's a celebration. He's OK with it."

"I'm not!" Sissy's face grew red. "It's taken us quite a while to get you to the point where you're working and sober during the day. I don't need you backsliding."

Duck responded sheepishly, "I'm not backsliding."

"Really? Really? Cause that's not what it looked like to me!" Sissy's forefinger stabbed toward his face as she spoke. "And what was that comment about you losing the race to Brody because you had water in your goggles?"

Duck looked up at the sky, exasperated. "That's what happened!"

Sissy continued to drive her point home with her forefinger. "Listen, Dean might believe that bullshit, but don't try that story on me!" Sissy turned away, took a deep breath, and exhaled, composing herself. She turned back to Duck, her voice more sympathetic. "Duck, you've got to get a grip on the truth. You can't continue to live a lie. You know it's a lie and yet you believe it. This is just one small example."

Duck stood speechless, bag of ice on his swollen jaw.

Sissy waited for a response, but there was none. "Fine!" she spit out as she stormed back into the restaurant in frustration.

Duck looked around, shrugged, and then headed toward the *Second Chance*. He was sure that he had another beer in the cooler on the boat.

Chapter 16

As Trista drove past the marina, two people appeared to be setting up for a broadcast next to a TV satellite truck parked in the gravel lot. The handsome young man in a stylish yellow rain jacket and jeans was gesturing toward the docked boats and the water beyond. The older man seemed to be disagreeing regarding camera angle as he motioned with both hands in a different direction. The body language and arm motions indicated that the disagreement continued as she viewed them in her rearview mirror.

Trista pulled up in front of her cottage and sat for a moment. She had difficulty getting over the disappointment of not being successful at the Coast Guard base. Eventually, she exited the car and dragged herself up the steps. Throwing her purse and keys on the coffee table, she slumped onto the sofa. In despair, she picked up the remote. After turning on the TV, she dropped the remote onto the sofa.

The announcer spoke solemnly. "This could be the storm of the century. Renee is now on a direct path to make landfall early Thursday morning on the Outer Banks of North Carolina." The graphic of the spaghetti models predicting the storm's path was superimposed on the screen. Most of the lines converged on the Outer Banks. One line brought the storm ashore near Myrtle Beach South Carolina. Another tracked the storm to the east of the coastline and then showed it swerving out to sea.

The announcer continued, moving his hand along the lines on the map. "All of these projections are based on the timing of the arrival of an upper-level cold front that will be dropping from Canada and steering the path of the hurricane." He swept his hand along the line that ran through South Carolina. "This model is based on an estimated late arrival of that cold front." Next, he traced the offshore line. "This model is based on the upper-level front arriving early and pushing the storm offshore before it has a chance to make landfall. However, most of the models show Renee hammering the North Carolina coast before it is pushed out to sea."

Trista, who had a glimmer of hope during the early part of the explanation, now sank back into the sofa in despair.

"Our correspondent, Will Franklin is on location in the Outer Banks." Trista recognized the reporter on the screen. He was the same man that she had seen in the marina parking lot.

"Tell us, Will, what's it like there right now?"

There was a bit of a delay as Will nodded his head. Then he spoke. "As you can see, Frank," he swept his hand toward the docked boats and water behind him, "it's all very calm here now. But this will all be changing very soon." He began walking as he spoke. "The residents of the Outer Banks are no strangers to the destructive force of hurricanes." Trista recognized the sign now behind the correspondent. It was the one that struck her with awe when she first entered the cafe. "This sign," he pointed up to the red line, "chronicles the sound-side flooding that swept through here during Hurricane Irene. It's a sobering reminder of the raw power of hurricanes." He paused and then shook his head in affected concern. "Based on current predictions, Renee will eclipse Irene in power. Some of the models show Renee coming up the sound just as Irene did." Pointing at the sign again, he commented somberly, "This sign may be a forgotten memory in the wake of Renee."

The studio newscaster, now on a split screen with Will, cut in. "Will is going to be broadcasting over the next few days to keep us up to date on the conditions there in the Outer Banks. Thanks, Will."

The handsome reporter nodded and then disappeared from the screen.

"Stay with us for the up-to-date coverage."

Trista shut off the TV in disgust and tossed the remote across the room. Exhausted, she sprawled out on the sofa. The string of sleepless nights and the day's empty drive all weighed on her. She closed her eyes for a few seconds. The seconds became hours as she drifted off into a deep sleep.

Groggy and disoriented, Trista sat up, searching the dark. She wasn't sure where she was or what time it was. Blinking to clear her head, she peered into the blackness. Slowly, she remembered falling asleep on the sofa. A touch of light filtered through the faint outline of the windows. What time was it? She looked in the direction of the TV to see the lighted display. It read 9:17. It was too dark to be that time in the morning, so it must be night. She shook her head, still trying to get her bearings. She must have slept for hours, yet she felt exhausted as if she'd fought her way free from the clutches of an overbearing tidal current. She felt something else, an empty, gnawing hunger. In her rush to hit the road, she hadn't eaten. She wanted to eat, but she also wanted to sleep. She forced herself up, giving in to the hunger.

Flipping the light switch, she squinted against the harsh glare of the fluorescent kitchen light. She opened the refrigerator. There wasn't much there, a half-empty bottle of milk, some cottage cheese, and some lunchmeat. Her stomach turned at the thought of eating lunch meat. She shut the door. Maybe she could try the café. They might be serving this late.

As she drove toward the restaurant along the dark, lonely road, she tried to remember what Emma had told her. *Ask for Jimbo? Was that it? Yeah, Jimbo.* Pulling into the gravel lot, she decided that she would give it a try. It couldn't hurt. She had to find someone willing to take her out on Thursday, storm or no storm.

Trista stopped short as she entered the restaurant. It was as if she had stepped through a portal to an alternate universe. It was the same room, but it was dimly lit. There were more people at the bar than at the tables and they were mostly men. Monday night football blared from the overhead TV and a chorus of groans and profanity exploded as the Panthers fumbled the ball. This was not a polo shirt and khaki crowd. She guessed that this jeans and t-shirt group consisted of mostly locals. She felt men's eyes on her as she started toward one of the tables. Without looking she knew that some were glaring at this intrusion and others undressed her as she passed. She was so uncomfortable that she almost turned around, but she was too proud to be driven off and too desperate to find a charter. She would stick it out.

She picked a table by the windows overlooking the marina and gazed out at the lights dancing on the water, avoiding eye contact with those who had not yet turned back to the game. She pretended not to notice the men studying her closely. A young woman, not much older than high school age, approached her with a pad and pencil. "Hi, I'm Jade. What can I get you tonight?"

Trista looked up at Jade. She was attractive but wore heavy eye shadow and liner. She was a slim woman but tried to create as many curves as possible with a tight low-cut knit top that displayed the cleavage created by her pushup bra. Her skin-tight jeans hugged her hips and thighs. Trista smiled. At least she wasn't the only woman in the place. "Are you still serving dinner?"

Jade cocked her head to one side and smiled. "We sure are. What would you like?"

Trista thought for a moment. She just wanted something simple. "How about a burger and some fries?"

Jade smiled. "Burger and fries. That's easy. What would you like to drink?"

"I'll just have water." Glancing around the room, Trista felt a bit uncomfortable and remembered how relaxed the wine had made her feel. As Jade turned to leave, Trista blurted, "Wait." This looked more like a beer crowd, but restaurants normally carried wine. Trista picked up the menu and scanned the beverage section. She found what she was looking for. "I'll have a glass of the Moscato." She knew nothing about wine pairings and was sure that it didn't go with burgers, but she didn't care. She liked the taste. Which of these beer-drinking, football-watching boys would know the difference?

As Jade wiggled her way past the groups of men, Trista watched her flirt with just about every one of them... and they flirted back. As she passed one table, she lightly ran her hand across a young man's shoulders. He grinned up appreciatively. As she passed another man, she pushed his hat forward over his eyes. He swatted blindly with his hand in the general direction of her rear end. She shifted her hips, easily causing him to miss. It was clear to Trista why Jade worked the evening shift. It was also very clear that these boys were very familiar with her. This was definitely a locals' hang out at night.

In little time at all, Jade had her wine at the table. Trista sipped on the glass as she looked out the window toward the gently rocking boats in their slips. It was hard to imagine that the rhythmic lullaby of the water would soon give way to a violent crashing creature.

The wine had warmed and mellowed her by the time her food arrived. She was feeling more confident now. As Jade set down the plate with her burger and fries, Trista spoke, "Emma told me to ask for Jimbo. Is he working tonight?"

Jade motioned with her head toward the bar. "He sure is. That's him behind the bar."

In the dimly lit restaurant, Trista could make out a large man serving up beer and loud commentary on the game. She'd not quite had enough liquid courage to approach him, but she ordered a second glass of wine and figured she'd be ready by the time she finished her meal. She was right.

Trista surveyed the dark bar. All she could see was men's backs. It was too dark to make out a lot of detail. There was one seat empty at the end of the bar nearest the door. The man sitting next to it seemed harmless. From the back, he appeared to be an older gentleman. He had thinning white hair and his frame was frail, almost lost in the baggy shirt and pants. The clothes had probably fit him when he was a younger man. The ravages of age, like strong currents on the shore, had washed away what could have been a once rock-solid body. He was hunched over his drink. Maybe it was the broken posture of old age or of drunkenness. At any rate, Trista didn't feel that she needed to worry about him hitting on her. She stood up and noticed that she was just a bit unsteady as she walked toward the empty seat. She was glad to sit down.

The old man next to her glanced up with empty, glazed eyes and then looked down at his drink. Jimbo slid over. "What can I get you?"

"I'll have a glass of Moscato."

"One glass of wine coming up."

He strode off to fill the order and was back in a second with her wine. As he placed the sparkling liquid before her, she spoke up. "Are you Jimbo?"

Jimbo's eyes narrowed. A bit cautiously, he responded, "That's me."

"Emma suggested that I talk to you. She said that you know everyone around here."

Jimbo's face relaxed once he heard Emma's name. "Not sure I know everyone, but I know lots of people. How can I help?"

Trista took a long sip of her third glass. "Well, I know this is going to sound crazy, but I'm looking for a charter to take me out on Thursday."

Jimbo chuckled, "You're right it does sound crazy. Have you been watching the weather?"

Trista nodded. "I know about the hurricane, but I've got to go out on Thursday." Her lower lip began to quiver as her voice trailed off. With a shaky hand, she took another long swallow of wine.

Jimbo could see her distress. "Have you called any of the charters?"

Trista nodded again, sniffling. "I got the numbers from the marina and called them all." At this point, Trista broke down and could barely get the next sentence out between sobs. "None... of them... will... go out." She was now sobbing uncontrollably, her shoulders heaving.

Jimbo looked around a bit uncomfortable, not knowing what to do. "Hey, hey, stop crying." It had little effect. "You can't expect people to risk their lives like that."

Trista continued to sob.

Glancing around, as if searching for help, and desperate to stop the crying, Jimbo said, "OK, I'll tell you what. I'll ask and see if anyone in here is willing to take you out on Thursday."

Trista's tears subsided, and through sniffles she said, "You would do that?"

Jimbo, relieved to see her calming down, exhaled, "Sure, but there's no guarantee, understand?"

Still sniffling, she nodded.

The football broadcast was at a commercial break. A beer segment with scantily clad women was running. Jimbo picked up the remote and ran the volume down. Immediately, the men in the place looked around to see what was going on. Jimbo's booming voice filled the room. "Listen up, you worthless drunks." He waited for the place to grow quiet. "This lady is desperate to charter a boat for Thursday. Any of you willing to help her

85

out?" Except for some scattered chuckling, the place was quiet. There was an awkward silence in the room.

Desperately afraid that her opportunity was slipping away, she turned around and loudly announced, "I'll pay three thousand dollars." The awkward silence continued. Tears began running down Trista's face. She tried to control the sobbing but couldn't stop it as she repeated, "Three thousand dollars... please?" Except for her sobbing the room was silent. Then from the dark, at the other end of the bar, a voice spoke up. "I'll take you out on Thursday."

Trista caught her breath, and her heart began racing. She heard several of the men laughing as she strained to peer into the darkness. Through the tears, she was barely able to make out a man at the other end of the bar with his glass of beer raised in salute. It was Duck. He repeated, "I'll take you on Thursday." Trista's heart sank.

She could tell from the scattered laughter that the other men felt the same way that she did, but maybe she could use this. She turned back to the men. "See, we've got one taker at three thousand. Anyone else? I'll raise it to three thousand five hundred." The laughter continued with no takers. "Four thousand?" Still only laughter. She couldn't go any higher. It would be a stretch for her to come up with that. Her shoulders slumped as she realized that Duck was her only taker. Just then, someone noticed that the game was back on, and the Panthers had scored. Shouting and hooting swept through the room as she was lost in the excitement.

Trista sat down, defeated.

At that moment, a large man entered the restaurant. She heard someone call out, "Hey, Beau, come to watch the game?"

The man that she had met the day before at the marina strode toward her calling back, "Nope, just here to get my old man."

Trista noticed Jimbo hurrying from the back of the bar to meet Beau and calling out, "Now, Beau, we don't want any trouble."

Still crossing the floor, Beau commented, "Relax, Jimbo. I'll settle my differences somewhere else. I'm just here to take my dad home."

Beau stepped up to the old man seated next to her and placed his hand on his frail arm. "Come on, Pops. Let's get you home. You shouldn't have to share the bar with my brother's murderer." Beau directed the last comment toward Duck's end of the bar. Trista looked down the bar. Duck's head hung like a scolded dog with its tail between its legs.

The old man wobbled as he stood, supported by his son's strong hands. Together they slowly made their way from the restaurant, the old man's unsteady gait being guided by his son.

Trista turned toward the bar to console herself with the remaining wine in her glass. As she sat feeling sorry for herself, she saw Duck stand to leave. Jimbo called out, "This is kind of early for you isn't it?"

Stretching, Duck spoke, "Yeah, I need some fresh air."

Jimbo nodded. "You want me to call Emma to come and pick you up?"

Duck placed money on the bar and said, "No, I'm OK. She's out with friends at a movie tonight and won't be back until late."

Jimbo called after him, "You be safe going home."

Without looking back, Duck gave a half-hearted wave as he stepped out the door.

Jimbo slipped over to Trista and said, "He's drunk, you know. He probably won't even remember tomorrow that he offered to take you out."

Trista nodded. "I know. Even if he did, I'd be afraid to go out on the water with Duck."

Jimbo's eyes narrowed. "You know him?"

Looking toward the door and then back to Jimbo, she exhaled with a twisted smile. "I've met him. That was enough."

Jimbo paused for a moment. "Look, I'm not crazy enough to go boating in a hurricane, but if I had to, I'd want Duck on board with me. That boy learned to swim about as early as he learned to walk. In fact, his grandpa once commented that he took to water like a duck. That nickname stuck. Fishing, boating, surfing, swimming, scuba diving... you name it. If you can do it in or on the water, Duck does it better than anyone I know. I bet if you cut him, he'd bleed seawater. Hell, he was a state champion swimmer in high school and probably could have been in the Olympics if he hadn't gone into the Coast Guard instead of going to college."

Trista cut Jimbo short. "Duck was in the Coast Guard?" She was focused now. "Was he ever stationed at Elizabeth City?"

Jimbo responded, "Yep, Elizabeth City, Atlantic City, and maybe Savannah."

Trista decided that she would have to pay Duck a visit tomorrow when he was sober. He might be able to give her some information on how to locate Jason. He probably still had contacts in the Coast Guard who could help. She was beginning to feel better, thinking that she might have a possible lead.

She finished her wine and thanked Jimbo for his help as she paid. None of the men noticed as she stepped a bit unsteadily toward the door. The Panthers had just thrown an interception and the men were shouting out in anguish as she slipped from the restaurant. She crossed the gravel to her car as tendrils of lightning lashed the sky.

Chapter 17

As Trista turned onto the dark, narrow road leading to her cottage, Jimbo's words played over and over again. "Look, I'm not crazy enough to go out in a hurricane, but if I had to, I'd want Duck on board with me." Maybe she was misjudging Duck. Maybe he was her only option. Ah, but Jimbo also said, "He's drunk, you know. He probably won't even remember tomorrow that he offered to take you out." And what about this thing about him murdering Beau's brother? Duck was just too much of a wild card. Just then the heavens opened, and rain hammered on the hood and roof of her car, creating an echoing, clattering sound inside. Trista turned the wipers on high with little effect. She could see only feet in front of the car.

As she rounded a turn in the road choked with thick shrubbery hugging the shoulder, a man on a bike emerged from the curtain of rain on the shoulder to her right. She hit her brakes, fishtailing as she swerved left to miss the cyclist. Headlights cut through the rain from the opposite direction, and Trista spun the wheel back, trying to thread the needle between the bicycle and the oncoming car. Just as she did, the bike rider, who was already weaving, veered into the front of her car. The rider crashed onto the hood, up the windshield, and off to the side of the road. The car wheels thumped over an object just as she brought the car to a stop. Trista's stomach churned at the thought that she had run over the rider.

Screaming, Trista jumped out into the pouring rain, searching for the cyclist in the shrubbery along the side of the road. Just as quickly as the rain began, it subsided to a drizzle. In the red glow of her taillights, she now made out a pair of legs extending from the vegetation onto the edge of the asphalt. In the foreground, lay a beach cruiser, the front rim twisted at an odd angle. As she ran toward the body shouting, she saw no movement. She hoped that the bike, and not the rider, was the thump she'd felt. The man was splayed out face down in the grass and dirt. Trista was horrified at the bloodstains smeared on the grass around the man's head. Pleading for him to be OK, she knelt to turn him over but pulled back as he moaned, his arms pushing up and twisting his body over to his side. The face was covered with mud and blood, but she was sure that it was Duck. He struggled to move, slowly rising to a sitting position with his legs bent and his arms wrapped around his knees. His head hung down almost onto his chest. He raised it slightly and shook it slowly as if trying to free it from dark cobwebs. He raised his head, blinking his glazed eyes in the direction of Trista who begged for forgiveness through her tears. After a moment, his eyes seemed to focus, and held up a shaky hand to quiet her. "I'm OK."

He didn't sound very convincing, and his face was obscured by blood. Trista sobbed, "You don't look OK. Blood's running down your face."

Still blinking and shaking his head, Duck swept the palm of one hand across his face and looked down at the bright red smear on it. "Wow." He was still struggling to regain clarity. He ran his fingers absently through his hair and said, "I think it's just a scalp wound. Probably not serious, but they bleed like a slasher movie." He gave a weak smile. He moved his legs and arms, testing their mobility. "Everything seems to be working OK." He attempted to stand, stumbled, and fell back to a sitting position. "Maybe you can give me a hand getting up."

Trista shook her head. "You need to see a doctor. I'll call for an ambulance to take you to the emergency room."

"Nope, I tell you I'm OK. Please just give me a hand getting up." He extended his arm, reaching toward her.

Trista stood her ground. "No." She pulled out her cell phone.

"Just like my sister! Why do women always want to tell men what to do?"

Trista's eyes flashed. "Because men always act like little boys."

Duck laughed. He'd regained his senses. "Fair enough. Let's compromise. Help me get home. We'll take a look in the light, and if we see anything bad, I'll go to the emergency room."

Trista wavered. His voice and movement did seem OK. Secretly, she hoped that this wouldn't need to be reported. She was sure she wouldn't pass a sobriety test. "It's a deal." She extended her hand and grasped Duck's as he struggled to his feet. He wobbled a bit as he stepped onto the roadway, wiping blood and dirt from his eyes.

Looking down at his bike, Duck exclaimed, "What did you do to my beach cruiser?" He seemed more concerned about the bike than he did about himself.

"I'm so sorry. I couldn't see you for the rain and the shrubs. Then the oncoming car…"

Duck looked up at her and smiled, realizing that she was becoming more upset. "It's just a bike. The front rim can be replaced." He paused for a moment to be sure that he had calmed her. "But she sure is a fine vehicle. Can you help me get her into your trunk?"

Trista popped the trunk and helped Duck slide the bike in with the twisted front wheel hanging out. She reached into the console of the car, pulled out a handful of napkins, and passed them to Duck. "Here. Use these to clean yourself up."

He stared at the thick stack of napkins in her trembling hand and commented dryly, "Do you steal napkins from fast food restaurants? 'Cause if you do, I'm not sure I trust you with my bike."

Trista laughed.

Duck smiled at his success in breaking the tension. He wiped away as much blood as he could and then used the napkins to apply pressure to the source of the bleeding.

As they navigated the dark road, Trista continued to apologize. "I'm so sorry about your bike. I promise I'll get it fixed."

Duck pulled the napkins away and looked at them to check the bleeding. "Yeah, I kind of need the bike. Ever since I lost my license, it's been my only transportation."

Trista naively commented, "You know, the DMV will replace a lost license."

Somberly, Duck corrected himself. "I probably wasn't clear. The court took my license. I was drunk and totaled my car." Duck fell silent.

Trista remembered what Emma had told her. "There was an accident. Several people died. One of them was his best friend from high school." She wanted to ask. She wanted to know why Beau called him a murderer, but she also remembered that Emma said that Duck refused to talk about it. She thought better of it and remained silent.

Changing the subject, Trista explored another topic that still haunted her. "Jimbo said something to me about you being in the Coast Guard a while back." She paused to see if he would respond. Glancing over, she could see Duck, bloody napkins held to his head, staring out the passenger side window. She decided to push on. "Were you ever stationed in Elizabeth City?"

Duck hesitated, not sure where this line of questioning was going. He responded, "Uh… Yeah, I was there for a while."

Trista's hope rose. She continued, "I'm trying to find a guy who was stationed there a while back, Petty Officer Jason Mallory. Do you know him?"

Duck continued to stare out the passenger side window. Trista could see his face reflected in the glass. He looked weary. "I did know him, but you're not going to find him."

Surprised, Trista blurted out, "Why not?"

"He's dead. Boating accident. He went down and never came up."

Once again, Trista's hopes were dashed. She exhaled audibly as her shoulders slumped.

Noticing, Duck continued without emotion, "Sorry for the bad news."

Duck looked over at Trista, who was visibly upset. He studied her closely as they drove along in silence.

Trista pulled into the drive leading up to Duck's cottage and shut off the car. He looked over at her and smiled. "Thanks for the ride. I've got it from here. I'll get my bike out, and you can go home and get some rest. Looks like you could use it."

Trista shook her head. "No! That wasn't the deal. We're going in here and make sure that you're OK. If not, you go to the emergency room." She shot Duck a stern look.

Still holding the wad of blood-soaked napkins to his head, he looked up toward the heavens and exclaimed, "Women!"

Continuing to bore a hole in Duck with her eyes, Trista shot back, "Men!"

Duck chuckled, "OK, we had a deal. Come on in so that we can end this argument, and we can both get on with our night."

After removing the bike from the trunk, Duck led her up the stairs into the cottage. "I apologize for the clutter. I just can't seem to get my sister to clean up my mess." Chuckling, Duck looked over at mirthless Trista who stood trembling. "Looks like you've had a rougher night than I have," he commented. "You were drinking Moscato at the restaurant, right? We've got some here. I'll get you a glass 'cause it looks like you could use it."

Trista knew that she had already had too much wine, but Duck was right. She was shaken and was having trouble composing herself. As he disappeared to get her a glass, she found herself feeling flattered that he was paying attention to her at the restaurant. She grew flushed at the thought and hoped that it didn't show.

Handing her the glass of sparkling wine, Duck said, "I'll get you a towel so you can dry your hair." He disappeared down the hall. Returning, he tossed her a towel saying, "Let me go get cleaned up so we can see the damage." He walked off down the hall. Trista ran the towel over her face and then her hair. As she sipped the cold wine and exhaled trying to calm herself, she heard a shower running down the hallway.

Minutes later, Duck appeared with wet hair and a towel wrapped around his waist. Trista blushed and looked away. "This isn't exactly what I had in mind."

"Well, you wanted to see if I was seriously hurt, so take a look." He held his arms out and turned slowly for her to inspect.

She continued looking away.

"Well, are you going to look? I'm covered."

Trista reluctantly turned back and watched as he did a slow 360. He had a muscular, athletic body. His shoulders were broad and the muscles in his arms were taut. His torso tapered toward his lean waist. Just what you would expect from a competitive swimmer. Not as cut as it probably was years ago, but still solid. The wine had her relaxed and feeling warm. She found herself enjoying the view more than inspecting for breaks and lacerations. The towel wrapped around him covered him from waist to knees but somehow seemed suggestive. She blushed again. "Yeah, I don't see any broken bones." She tried hard to steer her attention elsewhere.

"But you've got a nasty swollen, bruised area under your eye and the blood is still running down your face."

Duck reached up and gingerly touched his cheek just below his right eye. "You mean this? That happened at lunch today."

Trista commented, "At lunch? Well, you're just a walking disaster, aren't you?" She intended it as a joke but regretted it almost immediately.

Duck replied, "Yeah, that seems to be the common opinion."

Trista felt an uncomfortable shift in mood. She shifted the conversation. "Let me take a look at your head in the light." She stood up. "Sit here and let me have a closer look."

Duck still seemed to be feeling the effects of her comment. He sat down quietly. Trista took his chin gently in her left hand and moved his head while she ran the fingers of her right hand through his wet hair looking for the source of the bleeding. After a few seconds, she said, "There it is." She took the damp towel from around her shoulders and dabbed at his scalp. "That's it? That little cut is causing all this bleeding?"

Duck said, "Told you so."

She looked down to see Duck's eyes studying her. Nervously, she glanced back to the cut on his head.

"It looks like the bleeding is slowing. Do you have any gauze?"

Duck nodded, "I'll get it."

As Duck headed down the hall, she chuckled to herself and said beneath her breath, "I guess Jimbo was wrong. He doesn't bleed seawater."

He returned in a moment with a box of gauze pads and sat again. Trista opened several of the packets and doubled the gauze to make a thick layer. She located the cut again and placed the gauze on the spot. "Put your hand here and apply pressure," she commanded.

Duck raised his hand, but to her surprise, he placed it lightly on the back of her hand. "I've never had such a beautiful doctor take care of me."

Trista looked from the wound to find Duck's eyes searching hers. She hadn't noticed before, but they were a deep ocean blue. Her cheeks burned as blood rushed in a crimson blush. She felt a bit unsteady as if standing on the deck of a boat rocking on the waves. Adrift without a rudder in the depth of his eyes, she was being carried along with the surging tide. She felt his hand lightly run up her forearm and over the inside of her elbow as it moved to her upper arm. A chill swept over her as she closed her eyes. It had been such a long time since a man had touched her this way.

For some reason, being called beautiful by Duck meant more to her than her earlier exchange with the young man in the restaurant. Duck had been drinking heavily and he was, well… Duck. But for some reason, it felt sincere. She stood, eyes closed, her body tingling as his hand moved up and lightly caressed her neck. She shuddered. Without thinking, she looked down to find her hand caressing his face. She leaned forward and kissed him, gently, softly at first. The kiss became more passionate as Duck stood and pulled her to him. She was caught up in a rip current that was sweeping her out into dangerously deep water.

Chapter 18

Trista heard a voice in the distance. Through the mist, she could see a figure floating toward her partially shrouded by the haze. As the figure drew closer, she could make out a white flowing gown, dancing in the wind. It was a young girl. Her long hair also flowed in the breeze. The girl floated before her with outstretched arms reaching toward Trista. As the figure grew ever nearer, Trista could hear the voice calling distinctly, "Mommy. Where are you, Mommy?" She could now see the face of the young girl clearly. It was her nine-year-old daughter, Angie. She floated in the distance, wearing her white baptismal dress. As if being held captive by the mist, Angie came no closer. Trista caught a glimmer of light from below her daughter's neck. It was the necklace. The other half of the heart necklace gleamed in the mist. Angie pleaded again, "Mommy, where are you?"

Crestfallen, Trista called out, "I'm right here, baby."

Angie looked far beyond Trista into the distance and cried, "Mommy? Where are you, Mommy?"

Trista's tears streaked her face as she called out even louder, "I'm here, Angie. Can't you see me?"

Again, Angie called for her mother.

Trista reached out sobbing, unable to touch her daughter who continued to call for her mother.

Trista woke with a start, breathing heavily as tears streamed down her cheeks. Quietly she sobbed, "I'm coming, baby. I'm coming." She swept her fingers over her moist eyes and blinked, straining to see through the darkness. Like many nights before, Angie and the dream were gone, but something was different. What was that sound? It was a rasping, nasally growl. Snoring? But she was awake. She turned toward the sound to find Duck's naked body lying next to her in the bed. With fearful anticipation, she pulled back the sheets to find that she was naked as well. In exasperation and embarrassment, she looked up at the ceiling. What had she done? She had to get out of there. She slipped out of the bed as quietly as she could and searched in the dark for her clothes. She managed to find her damp blouse and shorts. She wasn't so lucky finding her bra and panties. She would worry about those later. Slipping the wet clothes on, she picked up her sandals and tiptoed barefoot through the cottage and onto the back deck. As she started down the steps, she was startled by a voice.

"Morning, Trista"

She gasped as she spun around. Emma sat in the moonlight, bottle of beer in hand.

"Sorry, didn't mean to scare you. I couldn't sleep, so…" Duck's sister held up the bottle before taking a swig.

Once again, Trista felt the warmth of the blood rushing to her face and hoped that it was too dark for Emma to notice. She struggled to find the right words. "It's not what it looks like… I mean, I hit Duck with my car… I mean, he's OK, but… and we both had too much to drink." She was stumbling over her own words. Her explanation didn't make sense and the more she talked the worse it got.

Sissy spoke up. "Yeah, I saw Duck's bike out front." A sly smile crept across her face. "But he seems to be doing fine."

"I'm so sorry, Emma—"

Sissy held up her hand. "First of all, call me Sissy. That's what all of Duck's friends call me. I'd say you qualify as one of his friends." She nodded. "Sorry, but after I saw his bike, I looked into his bedroom to make sure he was OK."

Trista's face felt hot from the crimson rising in her cheeks.

"Secondly, you just performed a miracle, so no apology is necessary."

"Miracle? What miracle?" Trista was lost.

Sissy smiled. "Except for being a bit protective of me, Duck hasn't felt anything for anyone in a long, long time. He obviously feels something for you. That, my dear, is a miracle. If it takes hitting him with your car to make that happen, then I'm all for it." Sissy chuckled.

Trista felt very uncomfortable. "Well, he was pretty drunk. I'm not sure that qualifies as 'having feelings' for someone."

Sissy looked up at the stars as if considering this last statement. "Well, Duck is often drunk, but he has never allowed a woman to get close to him. No, this is different."

Trista shook her head. "I'm not so sure. He was so drunk that he offered to take me out on his boat on Thursday."

Sissy bolted upright in her chair. "He what!"

Trista held up her hand to calm Sissy's fear. "Don't worry. He was so drunk that he won't even remember when he wakes up. I'm desperate, but not desperate enough to expect him to keep his drunken promise. I wouldn't put too much stock in anything he did or said tonight."

Sissy took a long swig of beer. "You don't know Duck like I do." She shook her head. "Thursday." Sissy sat in silence staring at the ocean. The lapse in the conversation became so awkward that Trista felt the need to leave. "Well, I better get back to my place. Good night or good morning." She waved and started down the steps.

Sissy spoke, "Aren't you forgetting something?"

Trista turned with a puzzled look.

"Your car is parked out front."

Trista exclaimed, "Ah, right." She hesitated for a second as she glanced at the cottage door and then at the tall dunes that separated the beach from the cottages. "I think I'll just walk around so that I don't wake Duck."

"Sounds like a plan."

Trista descended the stairs to the beach and walked through the sand along the dunes. Then she climbed the stairs leading to her cottage to cut through and retrieve her car out front. This trip just kept getting worse by the minute, and Angie continued to call to her.

Chapter 19

The starting tone and a clean entry. As Duck broke the surface of the water his rhythm was perfect, stroke, kick, breathing. Fluid motion and power combined in the breaststroke. He glanced to the side. Brody was in a zone. Stroke for stroke they matched each other. Then it happened. Duck glanced again to find Brody thrashing in the water. Then he sank from view. Duck continued toward the wall and made the turn. Up ahead, Brody broke the surface, gasping for air. Duck continued, perfect stroke, perfect breathing, perfect finish. He turned back. Brody's lane was empty. Duck dove below the lane markers, searching the bottom of the pool. Brody was nowhere. He swam upward. As he broke the surface and gasped for air, he found himself in a storm-tossed ocean. He treaded water searching for Brody in the waves.

Duck was jolted from his nightmare. Perspiration streamed down his face as he trembled in the dark. The nightmares were relentless. Each time, someone paid for Duck's failure. When others needed it most, the perfect Duck wasn't perfect.

As his breathing slowed and the pounding in his chest eased, he looked around the dark room. A sad smile crept across his face as he realized that he was alone. He stood and slipped on a t-shirt and shorts. Walking down the hall, he recognized Sissy's rattling snore as he passed her room. He moved through the kitchen and passed Fetch, asleep on the floor. Hearing the footfalls, the old dog raised his head. Duck opened the door and called back, "Come on, old boy. Let's go for our morning walk." Fetch rose and stretched. Duck waited at the open door. The two of them descended the steps to the beach and soon disappeared in the darkness along the shore. Duck hoped that one morning the walk would clear his conscience. Until now, it hadn't, but it beat tossing sleeplessly in bed for hours.

Chapter 20

Last night's storm clouds rose from the eastern horizon like insurmountable purple mountains. Early sunrise tinged their peaks in neon shades of pink and orange. Trista marveled at the beauty in the storm at a distance. She knew that she would soon see the monster beneath the beauty.

The pink and orange gave way to yellow as the sun cleared the tops of the mountainous clouds. The yellow light danced on the surface of the ocean. Trista watched the hypnotic light show until movement in her periphery woke her from the trance. Duck and Fetch were walking slowly up the beach and would soon pass where she sat on the deck of her cottage. She wanted to melt into the chair and become invisible. Duck looked out toward the sunrise on the horizon. She held her breath, hoping that he wouldn't turn and see her. He didn't. Duck and Fetch walked past. She exhaled in relief.

Suddenly, without thinking, she stood and ran down the steps. She felt compelled to tell him. She had to let him know that she wouldn't take his offer to charter on Thursday. Especially after what happened between them, she couldn't let him do that. It would look as if she slept with him to manipulate the situation.

Trista fought with her better judgment as she ran toward him, calling his name. Duck heard her voice over the roar of the waves and turned to see her running his way. She was out of breath when she reached him. She gasped for air and grasped for words. This led to an uncomfortable moment. Finally, her breathing recovered enough for her to get out, "I wanted to talk to you…"

Duck smiled. "About?" He could tell that Trista was uncomfortable. She was flushed and struggling to finish the sentence. Her lips moved trying to form the words and she avoided eye contact.

Now she wished that she'd listened to her better judgment because she hadn't prepared for this conversation. She wasn't sure what to say. "About last night…" She paused and glanced up at him.

Duck's expression reflected confusion.

Trista stumbled over her words. "I mean… you know…" She motioned between the two of them with the forefinger of one hand.

Duck shook his head, "No, I don't."

Trista felt her face, hot and bright red. She was really regretting her spur-of-the-moment decision. She continued to stumble. "You… me…"

Duck's expression was blank.

"Last night?" Trista was hoping that he would get it and help her out.

Duck looked puzzled. "Last night?" He chuckled. "Well, last night was one of the worst evenings of my drunken life. Can't remember a thing. I don't even know how I got home, but it must've been quite a trip 'cause my bike's a twisted mess this morning."

Trista exhaled as her taut muscles relaxed. She said a silent prayer of thanks when he said he didn't remember anything. Then a new embarrassment swept over her. Was his inability to remember due to some inadequacy on her part? She had often wondered if that had been a problem in her past relationship. She felt a mix of relief, embarrassment, and anger.

"So, what about last night?" Duck's eyes narrowed.

She had to say something. Might as well go straight to the point. "You told me that you'd take me out on your boat Thursday."

Duck's eyes went wide in surprise. "I did?"

"Yes, but you were drunk when you said it. I don't expect you to follow through with something when you obviously didn't know what you were saying."

Duck's expression became thoughtful. "That's very honorable." He glanced out at the ocean and then back to Trista, "... but I'm a man of my word. If I said it, I meant it, and I'll do it."

Trista didn't understand. She shook her head. "No, I just told you that I'm releasing you from your promise."

"I know, and I just told you that I'm keeping my word."

This wasn't going the way that Trista had expected. She couldn't believe that she was trying to talk someone out of the Thursday trip. "Why would you risk your life over a drunken comment?"

Duck chuckled. "I wouldn't. But I would take a calculated risk to help someone so desperate that she's willing to put her life on the line. You can quit looking. You've got your boat for Thursday."

Trista stammered, "I... I... Uh... don't want you to think that I'm not grateful but..."

"Then just say, 'Thank you.'" Duck flashed a boyish grin. There was something about it, so easy and calming. It drew her in despite her efforts to stay distant.

Trista stood speechless. Finally, she said, "Thank you?"

"You're welcome."

After an awkward, silent moment, Trista raised her hands, palms up and then dropped them to her sides, not knowing what to say. She turned and walked toward her cottage, her head spinning. What just happened? She was too stunned to celebrate.

Duck watched as she trudged through the loose sand. The effort taken to stride across the beach caused the muscles in her legs to tighten. He admired her lean and muscular legs as he followed their lines up her shapely torso. She was a beautiful woman. Duck smiled as he thought of how much more beautiful she was when she was lying next to him last night. As he turned to walk off, he winced and grabbed his chest on the left side. Massaging his ribs with his hand, he spoke quietly to Fetch. "You know, buddy, I'm pretty beat up this morning, but it was worth it." He ruffled the old dog's coat and glanced back over his shoulder toward Trista, wincing again as the twisting motion sent a stab of pain running just under his arm.

Chapter 21

Duck left the ocean behind as he stepped into the cottage with Fetch in tow. He'd only taken a few steps when he stopped and thought of turning back. Sissy sat at the table with a calculator and bills strewn all around her. Her elbows were planted firmly on the table, and her head hung heavily in her hands. Her expression was one of desperation. Duck hated these moments and knew that Sissy would be in a foul mood. There were always more bills than money to pay them. Hearing Duck enter, she raised her head, her hair disheveled from running her hands through it, hoping to force her brain to find a solution. Duck had seen this many times before and anticipated her next comment. Sissy looked tired. "Duck, I don't know how we're going to make it. We've got to have more money. You've got to do something more than work at the marina."

Duck looked down at his feet and wished that they were in the wash of the waves outside.

"Duck, when is all of this going to end?"

Duck wouldn't make eye contact. "All of what?"

"You know exactly what I'm talking about. When are you going to pick yourself up and get on with life?"

Duck shrugged and looked out the window toward the beach, wishing to be out there.

Fetch, worn out from the morning walk, had flopped onto the floor at Sissy's feet. Suddenly his head shot up. He growled, looking toward the front door at some unseen danger. Sissy and Duck's conversation ended as they exchanged shocked expressions. Fetch never growled. Duck thought that he had forgotten how or had become too old to exert the effort. Fetch rose slowly to his feet, his gaze fixed on the front door as he began barking. Duck headed toward the door. Before he could cross the room, someone banged repeatedly on the door. Swinging it open, Duck came face to face with Beau. Fetch stood by Duck, barking and growling.

Stepping back, Beau stared warily at the dog as he shouted, "Get that dog away from me."

Duck shot back, "You've got a lot of nerve showing up here. I ought to let him tear you apart." Duck knew this was an empty threat since Fetch had lost most of his teeth and probably couldn't see well enough to find Beau's leg. But Beau didn't know this. Fetch continued growling and barking. Evidently, Fetch didn't know it either.

"That's fine! If you'd rather lose that boat of yours, I'll leave!" Beau spat out the words before backing away, still eyeing Fetch.

From the table, Sissy shouted, "Wait!" She rose and joined Duck at the door. "Duck, take the dog out on the back deck."

"I'm not leaving you alone with this jerk."

Sissy turned, fire in her eyes. "Duck!" She let the heat of her stare work for a second. Her voice hammered out the next sentence. "Take the dog out back. I'll be OK."

Duck could feel the heat of the stare but stood glaring at Beau. He punctuated his next sentence with his pointing finger. "If you touch her, it will be the last time you touch anybody." He continued glaring at Beau.

Beau held up both hands. "This is just business."

Duck waited a moment for effect and then grabbed Fetch's collar. Tugging, he said, "Come on, boy." He dragged the dog, still growling, toward the back of the house. With his back to the door, he smiled. Beau's face didn't look too good. He must've run into something hard.

Sissy folded her arms and cocked her head with a hard expression. "OK, Beau, what do you want?"

"I want my money." His voice was harsh and cold.

"You'll get your damn money. We just don't have it right now, but you'll get it soon. Now, if that's it, I've got better things to do." Sissy turned.

"No, that's not it. I've heard the same story for months now. Do you know how far behind you are on payments?" He waited for a response. "Do you?"

Sissy turned back to face him. She shrugged. "Maybe fifty, sixty days."

"No, eighty-seven days to be exact. If you don't have the money by Friday, you'll be in default. I'll take possession of the boat and sell it to cover my losses."

"Your losses? You didn't loan us the money." Sissy's eyes blazed.

"No, but my father's business did, and I run the business now. I'll never understand why he loaned you and your mother that—"

"If you'd been anywhere around, maybe you would!" Her voice exploded like a wooden structure hit by gale-force winds.

Beau cursed. "Really… You think this is about you and me? I left that behind long ago."

Sissy raged, "Yeah, I know better than anyone *who* you left behind. You think I don't know that! You promised that you were coming back for me! You promised!" Hot tears of anger now streamed down her cheeks, and she trembled in hurt and anger. She was angry at Beau and angry at herself for crying in front of him.

Beau hung and shook his head. Looking up, he held up a hand and said, "Look, this is just business. I need the money and you owe it. I don't care how I get it."

"You'll get your damn money by Friday. Now, get off my property." With one swift motion, Sissy swung the door, slamming it in Beau's face.

Duck and Fetch walked in to find Sissy sobbing and angrily swiping at the tears running down her face.

Duck said consolingly, "I heard it all, Sis." He picked up a bill from the table, glanced at it, and tossed it back onto the pile with the others. "Look, why don't we just sell the boat, pay off Beau, and use the rest to help us get on top of our bills?" Sometimes Duck's timing wasn't the best. This was one of those times.

Sissy shouted, pointing her finger in his face, "Momma bought that boat to give you a second chance. Maybe you've got no respect for yourself, but you are not going to disrespect her by selling that boat. Do you understand?"

Duck quietly nodded. Sissy could be blunt and demanding, but he had never seen her this volatile.

"I need some air." Sissy stormed out the back and strode off down the beach.

Chapter 22

Trista stood motionless in the shower, letting the jets of warm water beat down on her head. Streams of water ran down her body. Maybe if she stood there long enough, last night would be completely washed away. She lifted her face toward the rushing water. Is that what she wanted? Did she really want to completely forget last night? There was something sweet about Duck if you could just get past his careless attitude. She stepped from the shower, feeling very torn. She'd finally been able to secure a boat for Thursday… but with Duck at the helm. His outward behavior was very different from the person that Jimbo described. Who was the real Duck? Could she count on him to come through in rough waters? She felt uneasy.

Trista toweled off and slipped into a set of baggy cotton pants and a loose-fitting cotton shirt. Still drying her hair, she wandered out to the great room and picked up the remote. She hadn't checked the weather since last night. The young newscaster from yesterday flashed onto the screen. "According to the latest estimates, this whole area could experience a ten-foot storm surge. That would be devastating." The camera panned to take in the marina and the boats. "Everything you see here could easily be destroyed in the path of this raging storm." The camera cut back to the young man. "We'll be here reporting live, documenting the devastation and the toll the storm takes on the lives of the residents. From North Carolina's Outer Banks, this is Will Franklin."

The shot returned to a handsome newscaster at a desk. His dark hair was swept back neatly, revealing streaks of gray. "And now we go to our meteorologist Dan Billings for an update on the progress of Hurricane Renee."

"Thanks, Tom." A stern-looking Dan turned toward the camera. "I can't emphasize enough how dangerous this storm is. At its current strength, if it makes landfall on the Outer Banks, as many of the models predict, we'll see vast devastation. This is a monster storm." The camera angle changed to show Dan superimposed over a satellite image of the coast and Renee spinning in the Atlantic. Dan motioned toward the pinwheel of clouds on the image. "As you can see, this storm extends over a huge area." The image behind Dan changed to a map displaying the spaghetti models of possible storm paths. "You can see that most models predict landfall along the North Carolina coast." He moved to the right to allow his hand to follow the easternmost path. "We're watching another weather system closely. There is an upper-level cold front diving down from Canada. One model has that system moving quickly and steering Renee out into the Atlantic without making landfall. That would be the best-case scenario. However, even then the coast could still experience hurricane force winds and destructive storm surge. We'll be watching this closely over the next forty-eight hours."

The camera shot switched back to the newscaster at the desk. "Thanks, Dan. We now go to our correspondent Rachel Martin reporting from the Norfolk Naval Base where preparations are underway to move ships out of port ahead of Renee's arrival."

Trista had heard enough. She switched off the TV and tossed the remote disgustedly. This was disturbing. Even the Navy was trying to avoid the storm. Was she crazy to be pressing for a Thursday trip? Wouldn't Friday work just as well? What was it he used to call her? Anal? Was she just being anal? She could clearly remember the last time that he'd called her that.

* * *

"Come on Trista. You're not still angry, are you? I said I was sorry. What more do you want me to do?" He stood, arms extended and hands

open as if offering himself. Trista had seen this before, the very same speech, the very same act. She was weary of his "out of sight, out of mind" attitude. After no response, he began pleading his case again. "Look, it was only one time. She meant nothing to me. You're the only woman I could ever love."

Trista shot him an angry, tear-filled glare as she pulled out the suitcase and tossed it onto the bed.

He continued to try to work her. "I'm here, aren't I? I'm not with her, so who do you think I love?"

Trista shouted back, "You love yourself. That's the only person you love. If you loved me, you wouldn't put me through this hell over and over again! I'm finished. I can't do this anymore!"

Next, he tried the consoling, soothing approach. "I know that I hurt you and I'm sorry. What can I do to show you that you're the only one? I want to prove my love." His voice had taken on a mellow tone, like that of a parent trying to calm the pain of a child's boo-boo.

Trista screamed through her tears, "You can't show me something that doesn't exist!"

Now, his voice took on a note of sarcasm. "Quit being anal. This is the real world, not your perfect imaginary world. People are imperfect, even you. You need to lighten up and learn to forgive." Then his voice became soothing. "Now, put away that suitcase. You're not going anywhere."

Trista flipped the suitcase open, glared at him, and in a sarcastic tone replied, "You're right. I'm not going anywhere. You are. Now, pack and get out!"

*   *   *

She wiped away the tears. Even years after, this was a painful memory. Trista lifted a large leather-bound book from the coffee table in front of her. She slowly, lightly ran her fingers over the gold embossed lettering on the cover – ANGELA. She opened the cover to a color 8x10 of a beaming Angie on her baptism day in her beautiful white gown. Her silver half-heart necklace gleamed in the light. Trista touched the picture, gently running her fingers over Angie's face, caressing her daughter. Tears streamed down her cheeks.

On the next page, a smiling mother and daughter, heads nestled lovingly together, displayed their matching necklaces. This had been one of Angie's favorite photos. As Trista studied the happy faces, she absently ran her fingers over the etched surface of the necklace that hung just above her heart.

Page after page brought back bitter-sweet memories. There were more photos of Angie, some with her mother. There were newspaper clippings and printouts of web articles. One prominently displayed a picture of the marina and the café. The last page was a map of the North Carolina coastline. A small hand-drawn heart floated just offshore. Trista studied each page reverently, giving the attention deserved by a weighty topic.

She closed the book and held it to her bosom, lovingly caressing the leather. She let her tears run freely. This was a time to love and a time to cry. No, she wasn't being anal. Angie deserved to have things done right. Just "making do" wouldn't be good enough. Angie was calling to her mother, and Trista wouldn't abandon her. She would be there… or die trying. She did feel guilty about Duck's involvement, but he was a grown man making his own decision. After all, she would pay him well. Closing her eyes, Trista curled up on the sofa, clutching to her breast all that she had left of her daughter.

Chapter 23

Sissy's shoes crunched and crackled in the gravel as she crossed from the café to the marina office. Movement at the end of the dock caught her attention. She turned her head just as an orange life vest flew out of the cabin of the *Second Chance*. She stopped as a second vest catapulted onto the deck. She changed direction, accelerating her pace, to see who was trashing her brother's boat. As she drew closer, a third orange life vest came flying out the door. Sissy stepped onto the boat. The deck was littered with empty bottles, life vests, fishing, and diving gear. She peered into the dark doorway. Suddenly, she jumped back as an empty, airborne cooler whizzed past, inches from her face, and clattered onto the deck.

She shouted. "Duck! What are you doing?"

Duck emerged from the cabin, squinting in the sunlight. "Hey, Sis."

Still angry over the near miss with the cooler, Sissy demanded, "What is this mess?"

Duck looked at the deck strewn with equipment, junk, and rubbish. "I know it looks trashed, but I'm trying to get the cabin straight." Picking up a stale, half-eaten donut and throwing it to a frenzied group of squealing gulls, he shrugged. "Got to get all of the clutter out of there before I can stow things properly."

Sissy stood, mouth open, lips attempting to form words that she couldn't retrieve. Duck watched in amazement, Sissy speechless. The concept of Duck cleaning and straightening was mystifying... and suspicious. "So, what brought on this sudden fascination with tidiness?"

Duck looked up at the flag above the marina. It fluttered and flapped, never coming to rest. Next, he looked out at the water. The surface, that yesterday rolled gently, was now choppy with small white caps. Duck commented absently, "The wind's picking up."

Sissy waited, as Duck intently watched the waves. "You still haven't answered my question. What's with the sudden interest in cleaning?"

Duck turned back to Sissy with an incredulous look. "I can't take her out in rough water with all that loose junk in the cabin. It would shift and fly around."

There it was, the answer that Sissy didn't want to hear. Half in fear and half in anger, Sissy blew up. "You're not really thinking of taking this boat out on Thursday, are you? That's just suicidal."

Duck's eyes narrowed. "Maybe it is, but I made a promise and I'm sticking to it."

The needle on Sissy's anger meter jumped from the red zone to off the gauge. Her face was flushed as she shouted, "Just because you slept with the woman, doesn't mean— "

"This has nothing to do with what happened last night!"

"Then why are you doing this?"

The anger in Duck's eyes softened. He exhaled slowly, glanced out at the dancing water, and then back at Sissy. "Because it's Thursday."

"Because, what?" Sissy looked stunned.

"Thursday!" Duck's anger was rising. "Maybe you've forgotten what this Thursday is, but I haven't. I can't!"

Sissy's face and voice softened as she looked away from Duck toward the water. "I haven't forgotten." How could she? Tears welled up in her eyes. She blinked them back, not wanting to cry.

"Look, Sis, I don't know Trista's demons, but it's clear that she's driven by them. Trust me. I know the feeling. If I can help her face them

116

down, then I will. I'm through living with mine. I won't live like this anymore. I can't think of a better day than Thursday to come face-to-face with my own demons." Breaking the awkward silence, Duck followed with, "You know, two birds with one stone…"

Sissy fell silent as she continued to avoid eye contact with Duck. The tears she had tried to fight back were now streaming down her face despite her attempts to wipe them away with both hands. She hated herself for crying and then felt guilty for wanting to be the kind of hard-hearted person who wouldn't cry.

Duck's mood softened. "I'm sorry, Sis, but this is something I've got to do."

Sissy nodded quietly, still looking away.

"I've got to finish up here. I want to take her out today and see how she handles." He disappeared into the cabin, leaving Sissy on the deck. A second later, he popped out grinning. "Hey, Sis?"

She turned toward Duck with a pained smile.

"Thanks for running the outboards."

Sissy's expression twisted into a smirk as she realized why he was thanking her. Early on, when it became apparent that Duck wasn't going to take the boat any farther than the pier, Sissy occasionally slipped down and started up the engines to let them run for a few minutes. She just didn't want them sitting idle for long periods of time. She thought that she and Cap were the only ones who knew. She chuckled under her breath. "You're welcome."

Once again, Duck disappeared.

Tears streamed silently down her face, tears of anger, tears of sorrow… and tears of joy. In this moment, she had a glimpse of the real Duck – not the sorrowful clown that she had mothered for the past few years. This was the old Duck, focused, determined, and caring. In her joy was also the sorrow that she might not have him for long. In just a few days, he would take this small boat into the teeth of a monster storm. In all likelihood, he wouldn't return. Did he have to risk his life to help Trista? Did he really have to risk his life to regain it? Sadly, Sissy knew the answer was *Yes*. If he didn't, he wouldn't be the Duck she grew up with. That's who he was.

As she stepped onto the dock, she looked up toward the southeastern horizon. Menacing gray clouds hung low in the sky in dark contrast to the bright sunshine overhead. These were the first bands of clouds that would herald Renee's arrival. The storm was coming.

Chapter 24

Duck throttled back as he approached the marina's dock. For the first time, he saw the *Second Chance* as more than just a place to sit and drink beer as he watched the sunset over the sound. She handled nicely, quick response to the throttle and the wheel. That would be important in rough water.

Duck drifted up to the dock and tied off. Looking up, he noticed Cap standing halfway down the dock, watching him with a huge grin on his face. As Duck jumped off the boat, Cap strode toward him, beaming.

"Well, how did she run?"

Duck nodded with a smile on his face. Looking back at the *Second Chance*, he commented, "Very nice."

Cap slapped him on the shoulder, still beaming, as they walked from the *Second Chance* toward the café at the foot of the dock. Cap commented, "That's great news."

Duck knew that there was much more in the old man's comment than how the boat handled.

Looking up the dock, the two men could see a TV crew in the gravel lot. A handsome, young reporter stood, casually talking to another member of the crew who held a camera. Although the late-day sky was clear, the reporter wore an expensive-looking, bright yellow rain jacket. He stood with his back toward the approaching men. Cap and Duck overheard the conversation as they drew near.

The reporter spoke loudly, "We'll talk to a few people to get some local color on tape for tonight. You know, show the human side."

The cameraman nodded.

The reporter continued, "I'm telling you this is going to be huge. We're going to be here in the middle of the destruction... and the best part is we'll be broadcasting nationally. This is my ticket to a job in a bigger market." He chuckled, almost giddy.

Duck jabbed his elbow at Cap. When the old man glanced over, Duck winked. Cap wasn't sure what Duck had in mind, but he began to feel uneasy. As the two men drew closer, the cameraman motioned toward them. The reporter turned and, seeing Duck and Cap nearing him, pulled up his microphone. The cameraman focused in on the three men. The reporter called out, "Will Franklin with News Flash. Have you got a minute for a few questions?"

Cap shook his head, but Duck spoke up, "Sure, is this live?" He looked at the camera and smiled.

The reporter shook his head, "No, we're taping for use on the eleven o'clock news tonight."

Duck nodded, still smiling, "OK, that's great."

The reporter nodded to the cameraman and then turned speaking into the mic. "This is Will Franklin on North Carolina's Outer Banks. Last night, officials announced a voluntary evacuation for the counties of Carteret, Hyde, Dare, Camden, and Currituck. Here in Dare County, we're getting the reactions of people to this announcement. What do you think about the voluntary evacuation? Do you plan on leaving ahead of the storm?" He held the microphone out toward Duck and Cap.

Cap was silent.

Duck's smile disappeared and confusion swept across his face. "Evacuate? Why?"

Not expecting that reaction, the reporter smiled nervously. "The voluntary evacuation order for Dare County."

Duck chuckled. "Didn't you hear the most recent update from the National Hurricane Center?"

There was a brief pause with the reporter looking more uneasy. Then he quizzed tentatively, "Latest update?"

"Yeah." Duck continued, "The storm changed course. They say it's going to make landfall near the Georgia – South Carolina border."

"What?"

"Yeah, I thought you guys were on top of this stuff." Duck shook his head in disbelief.

The reporter motioned to the cameraman to stop recording. It was as if Duck and Cap no longer existed. The reporter let out a string of profanities and said in disgust, "Hundreds of miles from ground zero. There goes our story."

Duck and Cap continued walking toward the café. Duck's low chuckle escalated into raucous laughter as Cap joined in. The reporter turned toward the commotion.

Cap gasped, nearly choking on the words through his laughter. "South Carolina. That's a good one."

The reporter looked at his watch. "The next update isn't due for hours!" He glanced back at the two men who struggled to catch their breath as they climbed the stairs to the café. He let out another string of profanities. Turning to the cameraman, he demanded, "Erase that piece!"

The cameraman chuckled, "Why? It's not going to air."

"Erase it!"

Chapter 25

Trista woke with a start, tears streaming down her face. Just as so many times in the past, Angie had pleaded tearfully, "Mommy? Where are you, Mommy?"

Quietly, Trista promised in the dark, "I'm coming, baby." She sat up trying to clear her head. She glanced at the digital clock burning through the darkness, 8:17. She must have slept through the afternoon. The exhaustion from a string of sleepless nights had finally caught up with her.

Blinking and straining to see through the dark, she stood and moved toward the kitchen. A high-pitched squeal cut through the dark as she stepped, twisting her ankle on some unseen object. Stumbling backward, she fell onto the sofa. As she sat up, her heart racing, she made out the dark form of a dog, head up and paws splayed out at the foot of the sofa. She glanced at the seaside door that was partially ajar. Because it had become such a pain to open, Trista hadn't completely shut it. Evidently, Fetch had wandered in while she was asleep. Trista made her way slowly in the dark to switch on a light. At this point, Fetch had recovered and was sprawled on the floor.

Trista called out, "Fetch, come!" Fetch lifted his head, glanced at Trista, and then returned to his previous position. Trista exhaled with frustration. She walked toward the refrigerator. As she opened the door, the old dog's head popped up. Fetch watched with interest as she rummaged around in the refrigerator. There was no meat. She had a container of cottage cheese. Maybe that would work. Lifting it from the shelf, she crossed the room under the watchful eye of the old dog. Opening the container, she held it out to Fetch. He sniffed the open container, snorted, and then laid his head back on the floor, unimpressed. Trista looked down in exasperation.

Frustrated, she glanced out the window. Lights were on in the cottage next door. Maybe Sissy or Duck could come and get the dog. She headed out the ocean side door. Fetch watched disinterestedly from the floor.

As she crossed in front of the neighboring cottage, Sissy's voice called out, "Hey, girl, how're you doing?"

Trista stopped in the sand below the deck. She peered through the dark to find Sissy sitting silhouetted against one of the brightly lit windows. "Sorry to bother you, but Fetch has wandered into my cottage. He doesn't seem to want to leave."

Sissy chuckled, "Sorry, we'll get him out." The screened windows of the cottage were open. Sissy yelled into the nearest one, "Duck." She waited for a response. There was none. Trista could faintly hear the TV weather broadcast drifting through the open window. Sissy yelled again a bit louder, "Duck."

This time Duck's voice responded, "What you need, Sis?"

"Come get your dog."

A second later, Duck appeared at the door, looking around the deck. "Where is he?"

Sissy pointed into the dark toward Trista, standing in the sand below, her arms crossed. "He's made himself at home at her place."

Duck hadn't noticed Trista until now and, in surprise, responded, "I'm so sorry. I'll get him. He gets lost so easily."

Sissy laughed, "Or he knows where to find lunchmeat."

Duck gave Sissy a puzzled glance.

"Don't worry about it. Just get the dog."

Duck shrugged and headed down the steps. He continued to apologize as he walked beside Trista through the loose sand that separated the two cottages.

"I'm really sorry. You know that it's just his old age."

Trista asked absently, "How old is he?"

"Not sure, exactly. We've only had him a few years. One morning, I was walking the beach just before dawn. He startled me when he came loping up from behind. I looked down and there he was, wet and muddy. He fell into a trot by my side. I just kept walking, figuring he would take off again, but he didn't. You would've thought that we had been friends forever. Not sure why he picked me to latch onto, but he followed me home and hasn't left my side since."

"Didn't he belong to someone?"

Duck shrugged, "Not that we could ever tell. He didn't have a collar. We contacted the SPCA and put up posters, but no one ever claimed him."

Trista shook her head in disbelief.

"At any rate, we took him in. Sissy didn't want to at first. Said we couldn't afford another mouth to feed." Duck chuckled. "He likes to eat."

Trista said. "I know."

Duck glanced over, confused at the comment.

She smiled. It was a real smile. Not the sarcastic twist of her mouth that he had seen in the past. She was even more beautiful when she smiled. He was so caught up that he stumbled, almost tripping over the first step leading to Trista's cottage.

She noticed and felt the blood rushing to her cheeks, grateful for the nighttime darkness. She tried with little success to cool the fire in her face before reaching the lighted doorway.

Stepping inside, Duck called to the dog lounging on the floor, "Come on, old boy. Let's go home."

Fetch lifted his head with little interest, then laid it back on the floor.

Duck shook his head. "I don't know what's going on with him. He's not usually like this." In a firmer voice, Duck called, "Fetch, come!"

The old dog shifted his eyes toward Duck and then slowly rose to his feet and stretched. He then lumbered over to Trista and nuzzled her hand, licking her palm. Days ago, she would have pulled away, but now, she found herself running her hand gently along the dog's head and neck.

Duck chuckled. "Well, what do you know? I think he likes you."

Trista was surprised to find herself smiling at the comment.

For a second time, Duck was swept up in her smile. Then, remembering why he made the trip over, he called again, "Fetch, come." The dog ambled over to Duck who affectionately ruffled his fur. "OK, old boy, let's go."

As Duck turned toward the door, Trista spoke, "Wait."

Duck stopped and turned back.

"We probably need to talk about where we're going on Thursday."

Duck nodded thoughtfully, and then responded, "Yeah, at some point." Patting Fetch's head, he said, "Let me get this lost thing home. Why don't you come on over and we can talk."

Trista nodded, and Duck grinned. She watched as he and Fetch disappeared into the darkness.

She turned and stood for a moment, looking down at the leather-bound book lying on the coffee table. Should she take the book or just the map? This was such a private matter for her. She was also sure that if she said too much, Duck would think that she was crazy. As she thought through what she was asking Duck to do, it sounded crazy to her. But Angie was calling. Trista couldn't abandon her. After struggling for a moment, she picked up the book. After all, she didn't have to show him the other pages. She didn't have to go all Twilight Zone on him. He just needed to know where to take the boat. She could handle the rest after that. With her entire life's purpose tucked under her arm, she headed out into the moonless, starless night.

As she neared the cottage, a light came on and Duck stepped onto the deck. "Come on up and have a seat." He motioned to a chair next to Sissy, who was still sitting outside.

Trista climbed the stairs a bit apprehensively, but she had to have this conversation. Might as well have it now. As she sat down, she placed the leather-bound book on the table between her and Sissy and Duck. Duck eyed the album quizzically. Before Trista could even begin, he asked, "Anyone want a beer?" The two women both declined. Duck responded, "Well, I'm getting one." He left the table and reappeared moments later, bottle in hand.

Duck sat and took a sip of beer. Looking across the table at Trista he said, "OK, tell me where we're going."

Trista opened the book to the last page and held it up for Sissy and Duck to see. There was the map of the North Carolina coastline with the hand-drawn heart just off the coast.

Duck commented, "Well, that gives me a general idea."

Trista shook her head. "No, general isn't good enough. We have to go to the exact location."

Duck took another swallow of beer. "No problem. Do you have the map coordinates?"

She was struggling with what to say next. She needed to show him the letter, but that really required an explanation. She panicked. She should have known that it wasn't going to be as simple as showing him the map. She drew in a deep breath and exhaled slowly as she flipped back to the cover. Already she could feel the tears coming. She opened to the first picture, "I guess I need to start at the beginning. This is my daughter Angie. The picture was taken on the day of her baptism. She was nine at the time." Sissy could see the book clearly. Duck slid his chair next to Sissy so he could look on. Trista turned the page to a close-up picture of the two necklaces. The inscription could be clearly read. "As a special gift, she chose these two necklaces for us." Tears escaped the corners of her eyes and trickled down her cheeks.

Trista flipped through a few more pages of pictures of Angie—dance recitals, vacations, school plays, and church activities. "This picture was taken just days before I lost her." The picture was one of a beautiful young teen, the necklace easily visible in the photo.

Duck reached over and turned the book so that he could get a better look.

Sissy glanced up at Duck. He was studying the picture carefully with an expression of horror. Trista was so caught up in her own sadness that she didn't notice. She moved the book back and began flipping through the clippings and web printouts as she told Angie's story.

"Angie's father and I had a troubled marriage. Eventually, we divorced. During one of his court-designated weekends with her, he decided to charter a boat out of this marina." She stopped on a clipping that showed the marina and *The One That Got Away Café*. "It looked like a nor'easter would cancel the trip, but my ex pressured the charter captain into going out despite weather advisories." She paused, trying to compose herself. "The boat went down in the storm. No one survived."

At this point, Trista was sobbing. Sissy placed her hand on her back and stroked it consolingly.

"This Thursday will be the fifth anniversary of my daughter's death." Trista, eyes closed, continued to sob.

Sissy's eyes grew wide as she glanced at Duck. He was no longer looking at the book. Instead, he held his half-full bottle of beer by the neck and swirled the liquid, intently studying the spinning sudsy froth that looked so much like bands of clouds circling the eye of a hurricane.

As her sobbing subsided, Trista continued. "For months, I've seen Angie in my dreams. She is standing before me, arms outstretched, crying for her mother." She paused and looked from Sissy to Duck, who was still absorbed in his private hurricane. "Maybe you think I'm crazy, but these necklaces were never meant to be apart." She lovingly touched the broken heart hung from her neck. "I have to go out Thursday and send this half to rest with the other, with my daughter."

Sissy didn't want to tell her that her daughter and the necklace were probably hundreds, if not thousands, of miles away, the unwilling passengers on the ever-changing tides and currents. What good would it do? If believing that the necklaces were reunited would bring her peace, then let her believe.

Without looking up from his personal storm, Duck said, "I don't think you're crazy. I'll see that you answer your daughter's call."

The story told, Trista turned the page to a letter on Coast Guard letterhead. "I wrote to the Coast Guard asking for a transcript of the distress call from the sinking charter boat. This letter includes the transcript." She placed her forefinger on the letter. "This indicates the map coordinates. That's your exact location." She looked up at Duck who was still absorbed in the swirling storm of beer.

He glanced briefly at the letter and said, "Got it."

After an awkward silence, Duck abruptly stood and announced, "I've got a long day tomorrow. Got to get ready for a wild date with Renee. I think I'll turn in." He nodded to Trista. "Goodnight." Then he disappeared into the cottage leaving the two women sharing surprised glances.

After another awkward pause, Trista gathered up her treasured book as she thanked Sissy for listening to her story. Sissy preferred raging to crying, but she couldn't help the tears that ran down her face. The two women said goodnight, and Trista melted into the darkness between the two beach houses.

Sissy rose and entered the cottage to find Duck standing, arms crossed, in front of a display of swim medals on the wall. His gaze was fixed on the only silver medal in the display. Sissy watched silently for a while and then spoke up, "Duck?"

There was no response.

"Duck, you've got to tell her."

Again, there was no response. Duck stood transfixed.

In the silence, the TV weather announcer could be heard saying, "This just in. The voluntary evacuation for counties in and around the Outer Banks has been modified to a mandatory evacuation. This comes just a little more than twenty-four hours before expected landfall." Sissy knew all too well the violent storm that was raging inside the still room. A moment later, she sadly headed down the hall to her bedroom, leaving Duck to quietly navigate his personal hurricane.

Chapter 26

Dawn came more as changes in shades of gray than in yellow sun and blue sky. Duck and Fetch walked along the beach that churned in rough waves. The water and sky met in a gray smear at the horizon. Suddenly, the sky opened, pelting the two with large drops of rain.

Trista, looking from the dry shelter of her cottage window, watched as the dog and the man walked unhurriedly along the beach. They strolled as if the heavy rain were sunshine pouring down. She knew her own demons but wondered what haunted Duck.

The rain ended as abruptly as it began. It would come again, or so said the weatherman on the TV. This was just the first of several rain bands in advance of the storm spinning out in the Atlantic.

"We're still watching this upper-level cold front pushing down from Canada." The weatherman motioned against the map in the backdrop. "There is some indication that it is moving faster than earlier predictions." The weatherman turned to face the camera. "Depending on the speed of this front, we could see the path of Renee altered." The backdrop map changed, showing the path of Renee cutting through the heart of the North Carolina coast and then pushing north and east, back into the Atlantic. "This shows the projected path if the cold front moves more slowly. Renee will make landfall as a Category 2 or Category 3 hurricane with sustained winds between 110 and 120 miles an hour before being steered out to sea by the plunging front. This would mean devastation for eastern North Carolina and southeast Virginia." The background map changed showing a different path. "If, however, this cold front moves more quickly, it could weaken the storm and push it out to sea without making landfall." The weatherman traced the storm track with his hand. "The North Carolina and

Virginia coastline would still feel strong winds, but they would be on the western side of the eye. These winds are not as destructive as the winds on the north and east of the eye." The weatherman faced the camera again. "This would be much more favorable and could dramatically reduce the extent of damage from the storm."

Trista watched intently as the camera shot transferred to the news anchorwoman. "Thank you, Dan. We, now, go live to Will Franklin who is reporting from North Carolina's Outer Banks. Will, it looks like the winds are picking up there." The image changed to a handsome reporter in a yellow rain jacket with *The One That Got Away Café* in the background. His hair danced in the wind.

"That's right Marsha. I'm here in Dare County, North Carolina where officials issued a mandatory evacuation order last night." He motioned to his right. "If you look down Highway 12, you can see a steady stream of cars leaving ahead of this monster storm." The camera swept to the left and focused on a string of slowly moving taillights crawling down the road.

Trista jumped at the sound of pounding on her front door. Will Franklin rattled on as she walked tentatively to the window and peered out. A white pickup truck sat in her driveway. The *Two Shores Realty* logo was painted on the door of the truck. That was the rental company that managed her cottage. Opening the door, she found a man in jeans and a *Two Shores Realty* t-shirt.

"Sorry, ma'am, I'm from the rental company. A mandatory evacuation has been issued for Dare County. You're going to have to leave."

Trista blinked as if she'd been struck in the head, leaving her disoriented. "But… I can't. I mean… I need to…"

"I'm sorry ma'am, but it's in your rental agreement. All renters must leave during a mandatory evacuation. I'll be back in an hour to secure the property. You'll need to be packed up to leave by then." He turned and headed down the steps.

Trista yelled, "Wait!" He continued down the stairs. "Wait! You don't understand." Her voice grew louder as she tried to get his attention.

Now at the truck, he looked up. "I'm really sorry, ma'am." He opened the door and slid in.

Trista screamed through her tears, "You can't do this! No! This can't be happening!" She broke down, sobbing as the truck backed out of the drive and sped off.

Sissy was headed out to help Jimbo stormproof the café. Hearing the loud commotion next door, she walked toward the neighboring cottage to find Trista in a heap on the stairs. Her head hung in her hands and her shoulders heaved with each ragged gasp as she wept.

Sissy called out as she approached, "Hey, girl, why all these tears? What's wrong?"

As Sissy reached the bottom of the stairs, she heard Trista muttering between her sobs, "This can't be happening. It can't be happening. I'm so close."

Sissy consoled her as she climbed the stairs. "Hold on. Things can't be that bad. What can't be happening?"

Trista continued to sob. "The evacuation… they're… they're making me leave."

"Ah, yeah. I forgot. Renters are required to leave." Sissy fell quiet. She struggled with her thoughts for a moment. If Trista left, then Duck would have no reason to brave the storm. No reason? No purpose. What would happen to her purpose-driven brother, the real Duck, the one she now saw glimmers of? Would he be crushed again by this new loss and sink into deeper despair?

Trista drew up into a ball, her arms wrapped around her knees and her head tucked inside. Sissy watched this hurting mother who was desperate for loving closure. She thought of Duck, a man desperate for redemption. She drew in a deep breath. Maybe Sissy would forever regret what she was about to say.

"Pack up your things and bring them over to our cottage. We have an extra bedroom."

Trista raised her head and blinked through her tears. "But don't you have to leave too?"

Sissy shook her head, "No, residents are allowed to make whatever foolish decisions they like. They just can't count on police, EMS, or firefighters being able to get to them to save them when their house blows apart or washes away."

Trista sat for a moment stunned by this sudden turn of events.

"Come on, girl. Get up. I'll help you get your things together and moved over. You can be my long-lost sister visiting from out of town."

Absently, Trista asked, "You have a sister?"

Sissy winked and said, "Now I do." She grabbed Trista's arm and guided her through the door.

Chapter 27

Duck drove the last nail in the sheet of plywood that now concealed one of the side windows of the cottage. He looked down from his perch on the extension ladder and cocked his head at the curious sight of Sissy and Trista struggling to pull suitcases across the sandy area between the two cottages. He called out, "Hey, Sis, what's up?"

"Come down here and give us a hand. Trista's staying with us tonight."

With a touch of confusion in his voice, he replied, "OK." He'd learned a long time ago that he didn't need to understand. He just needed to do what Sissy told him. On the ground, he picked up the two abandoned suitcases and carried them in.

As he stepped through the door, he heard Sissy's voice down the hall. "You can stay here in our mother's old room. We packed up her things several years ago, so the dresser drawers are empty. Make yourself at home."

Duck showed up in the bedroom doorway with the last two suitcases. Pointing, Sissy commanded, "Duck, put those over by the window." Sissy looked around. Satisfied that everything was in place, she announced, "I've got to go help Jimbo stormproof the café. If you need anything, just ask Duck. He'll be around here locking things down."

Trista grinned gratefully, "Thanks, again. I don't know what I'd do without the two of you."

Sissy played it off. "It's nothing. Just don't keep Duck from getting his work done." She winked at Trista as she turned and walked off down the hall. Trista's cheeks became flushed.

Duck ignored the comment as he glanced away. "Well, I've got to get back to covering the windows." He strode past her into the hallway.

Trista called after him. "Hey… Uh… Do you need any help?"

Duck stopped and turned, looking down at the floor. "Well, the only windows left are on the deck. I think I'm good." He turned and walked off down the hallway. Truthfully, having someone hold the plywood while he drove the nails would have been easier, but he would rather manage on his own.

Trista's smile barely broke horizontal as he walked away. She called out, "OK, but let me know if you need me." Her shoulders slumped as she watched him slip out the door.

Chapter 28

Sissy sat in her car looking out across the gravel lot. Beyond the half-empty boat slips, the wind whipped up the frenzied chop on the Currituck sound. It was a frantic slam dance of water, waves, and foam. As nasty as it looked, it was only going to get worse. Gray gulls, feathers ruffled in the wind, adorned the tops of most of the pilings. The sea birds squatted, facing into the wind. To Sissy, it looked like a court of loyal subjects waiting for the coming queen. The marsh grass along the shore bowed and swayed reverently in the gusts of wind.

She was distracted by movement on the deck of the café. Jimbo was lugging chairs across the wooden porch into the front door of the restaurant. Sissy, stepped from her car and called out, "Hey, I'll give you a hand."

As she reached the deck, Jimbo emerged for a second round of chairs. He grinned. "Thanks for coming in to help. I know you've got your own place to take care of."

Sissy grabbed two chairs and began dragging them toward the door. "Duck's got that covered. Him and his girlfriend."

Jimbo stopped in mid-stride, the table he was carrying clattered to the deck. "Girlfriend?"

Sissy pulled up short beside him. "Yeah, I hear you've met her."

Jimbo returned a blank stare.

"The lady was in here looking for a charter for tomorrow."

Jimbo shook his head and laughed, "Her? Yeah, we've met. I kinda feel sorry for her. She seems desperate, but it's not going to happen."

Sissy silently stared at Jimbo. His laughter trailed off. "No. Please tell me that Duck's not taking her out."

Sissy sighed, "He's hell-bent on going."

Jimbo grimaced. "I thought it was just the beer talking the other night."

"Maybe it was, but there's more to the story. Last night she told us why Thursday's so important." Sissy paused. "Her daughter was on the *Seamist* when it went down five years ago." Sissy could see the gears turning in Jimbo's brain.

"And Thursday is…"

Sissy finished the sentence for him, "the fifth anniversary of her daughter's death."

Jimbo let out a low whistle. "Fate must have a sick, twisted sense of humor." He considered his comment for a moment. "How's Duck taking all of this?"

Sissy shook her head. "I think he was sweet on her, but this latest news has thrown him for a loop. Either way, he's on a mission now."

Jimbo shook his head. "Well, that's new. I don't think I've seen him interested in anything except beer in quite a while."

Sissy sighed. "Yeah, it's a wonderful and terrible thing all at once." The corners of her mouth rose in a sarcastic smile. "Maybe fate does have a twisted sense of humor… and poor Duck is the butt of the joke."

Jimbo noticed a rising tide in Sissy's eyes. Tears always made him uncomfortable. He gruffly announced, "Well, we better finish getting these things inside. We still have windows to board and loose items to secure."

Sissy was grateful for the opportunity to change subjects and began dragging her chairs again. Once Jimbo was through the door and out of sight, she swiped quickly at both eyes before grabbing the chairs again and heading toward the café's doorway.

Chapter 29

Trista surveyed the simple bedroom. It was obvious that Duck spent little time in this room. Everything was neat and tidy, probably just the way his mother kept it when she was alive. On the top of the dresser was a simple wooden jewelry box and a mother's proud display of framed photographs. Trista picked each one up and studied it carefully, wondering what story each one told. Pictures were more than people posing and smiling. They were frozen moments from the stories of people's lives.

She picked up one photo of a teenage girl who looked a lot like Sissy. She wore a sparkling prom dress. Beside her stood a plainly dressed woman. Her bright smile showing through the lines and furrows of a hard life. So, this was mother and daughter on a special evening. There were probably several stories in this one photo. There would have been the shopping trip together to try on dress after dress, laughing at some, arguing over the neckline or hemline of others. And finally, there would be a mix of exhaustion and satisfaction as they found the perfect dress. The picture also told the story of scurrying around the day of the dance. Sissy and her friends getting together for nails, hair, and makeup – maybe here at her house. Her mother might have played the part of hostess, helper, and cheerleader, assuring a self-conscious teen of how beautiful she looked. There was probably another untold story. The one of a mother spending money she didn't have, knowing that she would struggle to make ends meet and that she would go without so that her daughter could have a magical evening. Yes, so many stories frozen in one moment.

Trista carefully placed the picture back on the dresser. She picked up one of the smaller suitcases and laid it on the bed. Opening it, she removed her leather-bound album. She flipped through the pages until she reached the one she had taken seconds before Angie left her for the last time. This photo told a much different story. To the casual observer, this would be the picture of a smiling teenage girl. They wouldn't catch the subtle, taunting tilt of her head. The, *Here's your pose*, defiant attitude that Trista had seen countless times. The casual observer wouldn't notice the slightly exaggerated, forced smile. Trista knew the fake smile all too well. It was her teenage daughter's passive-aggressive way of complying while not-so-secretly saying, "I hate you." Yes, there was a story in this picture.

*   *   *

Angie, cell phone in both hands, was engrossed in a text exchange with several friends. Her thumbs tapped quickly at the keyboard.

Trista stood above the open suitcase on the bed, holding the scant sections of a string bikini in each hand. "Angie, why are you packing a bathing suit? The water at the beach is too cold this time of year."

Angie rushed toward her mother, reaching for the bathing suit. "Mom! I had that all packed. Why are you going through my stuff?"

Trista jerked the two small pieces of the suit back just as Angie snatched at them. "I'm just trying to make sure that you have everything you need."

Hands held out demandingly, Angie stormed, "Come on, Mom. We're going to the beach. I need my bathing suit."

"Honey, you're not going to be able to get in the water. There's no need to take it."

"It's still warm during the day. I might want to lay out on the beach."

"Not in this bathing suit!"

In anger, Angie blurted, "Mom, stop being so… so… old. There's nothing wrong with it."

"Nothing wrong? Have you looked at yourself in—"

In frustration, Angie zipped up the suitcase, slammed it on the floor, and wheeled it out of the bedroom door.

Trista followed, her voice escalating. "Don't walk away from me! I'm talking to you!"

Angie stopped in the hallway, suitcase in hand, still facing away. Her head was cocked in that same defiant manner.

Trista demanded, "No, young lady, you look at me when I'm talking to you."

Angie turned but her contempt was palpable.

"That bathing suit is inappropriate and you're not taking it. I'll never understand why your dad let you buy it in the first place."

There it was, the igniter, the spark that fueled so many arguments between the two of them. Angie exploded. "You know, he's not always wrong, and you're not always right."

Trista threw back, "I know that but—"

"No, you don't. Every time he does something, it's wrong."

"That's not so—"

"Yes, it is! Look at this trip! For days you've been criticizing and complaining."

"Have you seen the weather report? It's not safe."

"No, you're just mad because Dad's spending time with me. He never does anything right in your eyes. No wonder he left you."

Trista exploded, "Left me? He left me?" She caught herself. She had never gone into the details of the separation and divorce with Angie. She wanted so badly to tell her daughter, but she let her frustration come out in tears rather than words. For better or worse, he was her father and Angie needed to respect him. Trista stood silently blinking back the tears. "I don't want to fight anymore. Go on out and wait for your father."

Trista spun and strode down the hallway. Angie, still fuming, watched her disappear through the bedroom door.

Minutes later, the sound of a car horn alerted Trista to the arrival of her ex-husband. She hurried out to the living room to find Angie opening the front door, suitcase in tow. "Wait, wait!" Trista called out. "I want a picture of you before you leave."

Angie turned and exhaled in exasperation. "Really, Mom? Dad's waiting."

"It'll only take a second. Come on. Give me a pose." Trista smiled weakly.

Angie's shoulders slumped as she cocked her head, her expression full of disdain.

"Come on Angie. Give me a smile."

Angie complied with a strained smile. Trista knew from past experience that this was the best that she would get. After a couple of shots with her phone, Trista said, "Thanks, Honey."

The smile Angie's smile evaporated as she wheeled the suitcase out the door. Trista called after her, "I love you." There was no response from the girl who hurried to the waiting car.

*   *   *

Trista teared up. That was the story of Angie's last photo. How many times had she wished that she had those last moments to do over? In the balance of life, love certainly outweighed those few scraps of cloth. But in the heat of the moment, Trista lost her perspective and lost her daughter to anger and bitterness. If she'd only known that she would also lose her to the storm.

Trista flipped back to the close-up photo of the two necklaces and ran her fingers over the words as if she could feel the grooves of the engraving.

Always Together – Never Apart

Mother – Daughter

Sharing One Heart

In Trista's dreams, Angie called to her. She might not be able to rewrite her last bitter moment with her daughter, but she could live a new one… one with a final act of love.

A crash outside the bedroom window startled Trista. A string of profanities followed. Rushing to the deck, she found Duck lifting a large piece of plywood and struggling to position it over one of the windows. He attempted to hold it in place by applying pressure with his hip while twisting to hold the nail with one hand and hammer with the other. Trista moved quickly and shoved her palms against the board, leaning in with her body. "Here, I've got it," she offered.

Duck moved back and drove a nail in the upper corner. Stepping around her, he nailed the other top corner in place. Without looking at her, he said, "Thanks, I've got it from here." He began driving a nail in one of the lower corners, ignoring Trista.

"I can help you with the others," she offered brightly.

Focusing on the task at hand, Duck responded, "Thanks, but I'm good."

She stood for a moment, feeling invisible, as Duck continued without any further acknowledgment. She had the uncomfortable feeling that something was wrong. But what? Had she said something or done something wrong?

After being ignored for a long, awkward moment, she started for the door.

Still devoting his attention to the hammer and the nail, Duck asked, "Did you bring a bathing suit with you?"

This odd question caught her off guard and she hesitated with her hand on the door. Finally, she responded, "Yeah, there's one in my suitcase."

Duck looked up from his work. "Do you mind if I see it?"

Things were getting stranger, and Trista began to feel uncomfortable. Incredulously, she asked, "You want me to model my swimsuit?"

Duck chuckled and smiled, seemingly amused by her question. "No, I just want to see the suit."

"Oh… OK, I'll go get it." Trista's mood changed in waves from relief, to confusion, to shame. She wasn't sure why he wanted to see her swimsuit, but after the relief of not having to model it, she felt hurt that he didn't want to see her in it. She knew this was probably a remnant of her impression in her last relationship that she was never good enough, never pretty enough. All these emotions swept over her as she moved through the cottage.

As she laid clothes out on the bed and retrieved the suit from the neatly folded pile, she felt embarrassed. Holding it up, she hesitated and wasn't sure that she wanted Duck to see it. It was very modest by today's standards. It was a two-piece, but not a skimpy bikini. Rather, the top, while form-fitting, covered her breasts and had substantial straps. She had a fear of waves pulling the top off, so she always chose a suit with straps. The bottom portion of the suit also covered her well. It was very plain, no strings, buckles, or other ornamentation. Feeling the heat and color rise in her cheeks, she exited onto the deck with the suit in hand. Apologetically, she remarked, "It's not much, but here it is."

Duck looked up and watched her twist it slowly so that he could see the front and back of both pieces. He remarked, "It's perfect. Thanks."

She stood for a moment, unsure of what to do. She wanted to ask what he meant and why this was important, but feeling the hot flush in her cheeks, she hurried inside, glad to end the conversation.

Back in the bedroom, she folded the swimsuit and put it away. Looking back at the dresser where she had been studying the family pictures, she noticed something that she'd missed earlier. Toward the back, there was one picture frame lying face down on the dresser. Picking it up, she held the photograph of two teenage boys. They had broad smiles and proudly held large fish, obviously displaying their catch of the day. One was Duck. Trista began wondering about the stories in this picture when something in the upper corner of the photo caught her attention. The two boys stood in front of a boat. Just over the other boy's shoulder and partly obscured by his head, the boat's name could be seen. It was clear that it was the *Seamist*. Trista felt as if she'd been punched in the stomach. Suddenly, she felt weak. Slumping onto the bed, photo in hand, her focus shifted from one boy to the next and back to the boat's name.

Outside, Duck wrestled with the sections of plywood, nailing them in place over each of the remaining windows. He could have used Trista's help, but he was uncomfortable around her. When she was just a woman desperate for help, things were much easier. But now…

Chapter 30

Soaking wet and carrying a soggy pizza box, Sissy stepped into a seemingly empty cottage. There was no sign of Duck or Trista. The plywood-covered windows cast an eerie darkness over the house in the late day's cloudy gloom. Outside, the wind whipped and gusted with sporadic fits of driving rain clattering against the roof and siding. Sissy flipped a light switch and scanned the empty room. She called out, "Duck?" There was no response. "Trista?"

From the dark hallway, Trista's voice called back, "I'm back here." A light went on in Trista's bedroom.

Sissy walked back and stood in the doorway. "Sorry, I didn't mean to wake you."

Trista sat on the side of the bed, Angie's leather-bound book in her arms. "I wasn't sleeping." Trista looked weary.

Sissy motioned down the hallway, "I brought pizza. Come have something to eat."

A sad smile crept across Trista's face. "Thanks, but I'm not hungry. You go ahead."

"OK, but if you change your mind, I'll be out here." Sissy waited, but there was no response from Trista. "Have you seen Duck?"

Trista shook her head. "He was outside the last time I saw him, but that was a while ago."

Sissy nodded. As she turned to leave, she glanced toward the dresser and paused noticing something out of place. It took a second to register, but she noticed the picture that should have been face down on the dresser.

It wasn't. Trista didn't notice the slight delay in Sissy's departure or the troubled expression on her face as she turned away.

Sissy wandered through the cottage, past the stack of deck furniture just inside the door, and onto the back deck. She found Duck sitting in the one chair remaining outside. He watched the rain pouring in curtains from the overhang just beyond. She broke the trancelike silence. "I'm going in to change into some dry clothes. There's pizza on the table if you're hungry."

Without looking up, Duck replied, "Thanks, Sis. Maybe later. I'm not really hungry."

Sissy knew he really wasn't here. He was somewhere in the past. She'd become used to these detached moments over the years. She shrugged and turned back into the cottage to change. On her way through the living room, she turned on the TV and walked off down the hallway. The ever-present coverage of the hurricane was playing out on the screen.

After changing, Sissy returned to find Trista intently watching the coverage of the storm. As Sissy opened the pizza box, she asked offhandedly, "Anything new with the hurricane?"

Without looking away from the coverage, Trista pointed to the screen, "Look."

Sissy turned to see the weatherman on the screen motioning along a line that swept up and away, just off the coast of North Carolina.

"… with this upper-level system steering Renee just off the coast of North Carolina. We're also beginning to see a sheering effect at the upper levels. The eye is less well-defined. The last readings show sustained winds of ninety-one miles per hour. That's down from earlier readings of one hundred and thirteen."

With her gaze still fixed on the screen, Trista, asked Sissy over her shoulder, "So, does that mean that the hurricane is going to miss us?"

"Not completely." Duck's voice behind the two women startled them. He stepped closer to the TV as the weatherman continued.

"While this is very good news for the Outer Banks of North Carolina, they are still going to experience damaging winds, heavy surf, and tidal flooding. The good news is that it doesn't appear that they will see the kind of damage that they experienced during Irene or Isabel."

Duck talked over the TV weatherman. "We'll be on the backside of the storm. The winds aren't as strong on the western side, but they'll still be whipping up the waves." Duck fell silent.

The graphic on the TV changed and a path with estimated times appeared. "The National Hurricane Center has released this projection for Renee over the next twenty-four hours. As you can see, the forward progress has slowed. We now expect it to arrive somewhere east of the Outer Banks late on Thursday."

Duck spoke over the broadcast again. "Looks like the winds will be most favorable as we're headed out. But they'll shift quickly, coming out of the north. That's not good news. Getting out will be difficult. Getting back will be even worse."

Trista looked back at Duck. His face reflected determination. She spoke up, "Can we do this?"

Without turning from the TV, Duck said, "We'll do it." He continued to gaze at the TV, avoiding eye contact with Trista. Then he turned and walked off down the hallway. Moments later he returned and handed Trista a small box.

"What's this?" she asked as she studied the box.

"It helps prevent motion sickness. Take one tablet tonight before going to bed."

Trista attempted to return the box to Duck. "I don't have problems with motion sickness. Even roller coasters don't bother me."

Duck left her extended arm, box in hand, hanging in midair. "You've never experienced anything like tomorrow's ride. Trust me. Take it."

Trista held the box out a second longer and then took it back. Suddenly, the TV screen went black, the lights flickered, and the cottage fell dark. Trista heard Duck's disembodied voice proclaim, "And so it begins."

Seconds later, Sissy with flashlight in hand was lighting several small candles. The candlelight sent dark, misshapen shadows dancing across the walls of the cottage.

Duck announced, "I'm turning in." Just before turning away, he added, "We'll head out at eight tomorrow morning. We should have as much light as we're going to get by then." He paused as if running through a checklist in his head. Looking at Trista as he hit an unchecked box, he said, "Oh yeah, put your swimsuit on for tomorrow's trip."

Trista looked at him quizzically. He just turned and waved as he walked off down the hallway. "Good night."

Trista looked over at Sissy who shrugged her shoulders, seemingly as lost as Trista.

The two women sat in the dark silence a few moments longer. Without the background noise of the TV, the rushing sound of the gusting wind outside the cottage became more apparent. Trista rose and declared, "I think I'll turn in. We've all got a long day tomorrow." The two women said their goodnights as Trista headed down the dark hallway.

Sissy, sat for a while watching the shadows dance on the walls to the halting whistle of the woodwind chorus playing just outside the little cottage. The wind was picking up. As she blew out the candles, she doubted that any of them would get much sleep.

Trista lay in the darkness, her eyes wide open. She slipped earbuds in and pulled up one of her favorite playlists. As the music washed over her, she closed her eyes. She worried. Something was wrong. She couldn't put her finger on it, but Duck was different. He seemed distant. He'd hardly spoken to her in the last twenty-four hours and seemed to be avoiding her. She kept playing back conversations, looking for the offending word or the phrase. It was funny, but she actually cared. It bothered her that she might have hurt him. As silly as it seemed, she found herself thinking of him during the last couple of days. Out of nowhere, she would remember him studying her with his blue eyes, or turning slowly, his muscular torso wrapped in a towel, or even making his goofy comment about stealing napkins. Was he getting too close? Was she driving him away?

Her ex-husband accused her of pushing people away. He made the point over and over that she was the reason that their marriage fell apart. She drove him to other women. Could he have been right? Did she push everyone away? Did she sabotage her marriage, and was she now doing the same with Duck? Her eyes grew moist. No, she had done nothing wrong. Her ex tried to burden her with guilt to hide his own failings. Nothing was ever his fault. Still, Trista couldn't be sure. Maybe that's the reason that Angie always defended her father. Did Angie see it too?

Maybe she did the same with Angie. Maybe that's why they argued so much in her last year. Why did her last moments with Angie have to be so heated? Why? If she could only live those thirty minutes of her life over again. If she could just hold her daughter close and tell her that she loved her. But she couldn't, and it was like a knife in her heart. Tomorrow she'd try to remove the knife. She'd show Angie how much she loved her. Lying on the bed, Trista clutched the sheets in her hands so tightly that her fingers ached.

Outside, the wind wailed, and the rain rattled on the plywood shutters. Inside, Trista wept.

Chapter 31

Duck was the first person stirring in the dark cottage. The plywood-girded windows let in little light. From the faint flicker of candlelight in the hallway, Trista knew that the power was still out. She lay in the dark, listening. Outside, the wind howled in fitful gusts, and waves of torrential rain clattered on the roof and scratched at the plywood shutters. It was as if some creature prowled over and around the little cottage, trying desperately to claw its way in.

Remembering Duck's instructions, Trista rose, closed the bedroom door, and slipped into her bathing suit in the blackness of her room. Adding a beach cover-up, she opened the door and followed the flickering light down the hallway.

Duck's shadow moved like an animated giant on the dim walls of the cottage. Trista's first impression was that he was dressed like a puppeteer. His hands and face were visible in the candlelight, but his body was darkly clad and blended into the blackness of the room. As her eyes adjusted to the light, she realized that Duck was wearing a black wetsuit, creating this illusion. From behind her in the hallway, Sissy asked, "Are you about ready for me to take you to the boat?"

"Almost. We still need to get Trista ready."

Duck stepped over to Trista, studying her. "You're about the same size as Sissy. I think her wetsuit will fit you. Have you ever worn one before?"

Concern swept across Trista's face. "Why do I need a wetsuit? I don't know how to scuba dive!"

Duck chuckled, "It's not a scuba suit. It's for surfing… and, no, you're not going to surf either."

Trista's concern was evident in the troubled expression on her face.

The amusement disappeared from Duck's voice. "In this weather, I give us a fifty percent chance of making it to the place where the *Seamist* went down. I give us a ten percent chance of getting back to the marina with the boat under our feet." He paused. "But then I'm an optimist." Duck wasn't sure if it was optimism or fantasy, but hope had been such uncharted waters for him recently that he was having difficulty navigating them.

Trista still looked confused.

Duck continued, "If we… correction, when we get in trouble, we'll call the Coast Guard. They're good, but they're not perfect." Duck's voice trailed off as he looked away into the darkness.

Watching him closely, Sissy caught his hesitation and picked up. "The wetsuit extends the time you can spend in the water before hypothermia sets in. It increases your survivability."

At this point, Duck had recovered and added, "We'll just be specks in a great big, nasty, churning sea. Sometimes finding a speck in the ocean takes time."

Trista nodded somberly. "Got it. No, I've never worn a wetsuit."

Duck motioned to Sissy. "Getting into a wetsuit for the first time can be a bit tricky. Sissy will help you put it on over your swimsuit."

Flashlight in hand, Sissy called for Trista to follow her back down the hallway. Moments later, Trista returned, wearing Sissy's dark wetsuit.

Sissy smiled at Duck. "It fits her well. You were right. She is about my size."

Duck nodded. "Well, I guess we're ready." Looking at Trista, he asked, "Do you have the necklace?"

She nodded and touched the wet suit just below the neckline.

Duck shook his head. "That's not going to work in these rough conditions. Getting it out of there might be impossible." He handed her a small neoprene pouch with a carabineer clip on the corner and a Velcro closure running along one side. "Place it in here. It will be easier and quicker to get to when the time comes."

Trista pulled the necklace out of the neckline of her wetsuit, released the clasp, and lowered it into the pouch.

Clapping his hands and heading toward the door, Duck said, "OK, let's do this."

Trista shouted, "Wait."

Duck turned to see her disappear down the dark hallway. Seconds later, she returned with an envelope in her hand. Reaching it toward Duck, she explained, "It's all here, the four thousand dollars."

Duck stood, staring at the envelope.

"You know, the charter fee."

Shaking his head, Duck replied, "I don't want your money. I'm doing this for you, not for your money."

Trista waved the envelope as she spoke. "The other day you said you were taking me out because you're a man of your word. Well, show me the same respect. I said I would pay four thousand dollars, and I intend to keep my promise."

Duck wanted to end the discussion and get to the boat, so he moved for a compromise. "OK, but I agreed to three thousand, not four. You only offered four thousand because you hoped someone else would take you up on your offer… and save you from me."

Embarrassed, Trista blushed, but then her eyes narrowed as she considered Duck's comment. "I thought you said that you didn't remember what happened Monday night."

Duck flashed a crooked smile, realizing that he'd just stumbled over his own lie. "We'll haggle over the amount later. Give the money to Sissy. She doesn't let me handle the finances." He turned and headed toward the door.

Trista stood motionless as she studied Duck, wondering what else he remembered.

Realizing that she wasn't behind him, Duck turned and motioned. "Come on. Every second we wait the wind gets stronger, and the waves get bigger."

Trista handed the envelope to Sissy who stood by the door holding what looked like a walkie-talkie. Motioning toward the device, Trista asked, "What's that for?"

Trista held up the black radio. "It's a portable VHF radio. I'll be monitoring channel 16. If you send out a distress call, I'll hear it."

Trista gave Sissy a silent, sober glance. The dangerous nature of this trip was just now beginning to set in.

Just before Sissy stepped out the door, she folded the envelope and stuffed it deep in her jeans pocket. Carrying that much money made her nervous.

Outside the cottage, the wind gusted, sending horizontal streaks of rain peppering the three as they made their way to Sissy's jeep. Occasionally, they staggered against the bursts of wind. The driving rain pelted Trista's face like the stings of a swarm of angry bees.

The drive to the marina was quiet except for the sound of the rain hammering on the windshield and roof of the car. The heavy rain made it almost impossible to see, and Sissy crawled along as a result. Trista had a momentary flashback to Monday night's drive and collision. There was Duck's blood-stained body lying in the mud. Then in an instant, it was no longer lying in the mud, but floating in the waves and wash of the ocean. She shuddered, the image lost, as Duck commented. "The road's beginning to flood." Through the curtain of rain, Trista could faintly see the ponding rainwater, spilling small streams and pools out onto the asphalt. Duck added, "We're lucky that this thing is hitting at low tide, or it could be even worse."

As Sissy's jeep turned into the gravel lot of the marina, Trista watched a TV satellite broadcast truck slow and stop out on the roadway. She had the impression that the occupants were watching them as they emerged from the car and headed down the dock. They walked past the empty slips of fortunate individuals who had moved their boats inland. In other slips, boats bounced and jumped in a strange non-rhythmic dance.

As they arrived at the *Second Chance*, Trista's eyes grew wide. She spoke above the gusting wind, "Is this the boat?"

Duck yelled, "Yep, this is it."

Trista looked at the larger boats in the slips behind her and then back at the *Second Chance*.

Duck guessed what was going through her mind and commented, "They're all just specks in the ocean."

Trista smiled weakly. She wasn't so sure. She took Duck's hand as he helped her from the dock onto the unpredictably rocking boat.

Saying, "We'll need these," he picked up two orange life vests and passed one to her. Once Duck had his on, he checked Trista's straps to be sure they were snug. Then he clipped the pouch holding the necklace to a ring on Trista's life vest and directed her to one of the seats.

"Hold on tight. This is going to be a wild ride."

He started up the engines as Sissy cast off the lines from the dock.

Above the wailing wind, Sissy heard a loud voice behind her. "Duck, what the hell are you doing with my boat!" She spun around to see Beau rushing down the dock toward the *Second Chance*. They must have had the unfortunate timing of arriving at the marina while Beau was there securing his *Blue Water* boat.

Now running, Beau screamed, "Duck, stop!"

Duck had not yet pulled away from the dock, and Beau was only steps away from landing on the deck of the boat. As he passed Sissy, she lunged toward him, throwing all her weight into him as she pushed with her arms. Caught off guard, Beau stumbled to the side and fell into the thrashing water of an empty slip near the end of the dock. As he broke the surface of the water, he let out a mix of profanities and gasps.

Duck throttled up the little boat and, waving to Sissy, pulled away from the dock.

Trista, who'd watched Sissy blindside Beau, asked, "What was that about?"

Duck commented, "Well, technically this boat is part his." He shrugged. I guess he doesn't want to lose it in the storm." A slow smile crept across his face.

Knowing that Beau would be out of the water soon, Sissy turned and strode down the dock. Near the parking lot, a TV crew scrambled to set up for a shot. As she drew near, she heard the reporter, his back toward her, yelling above the wind. "Make sure that you get the boat in the shot behind me. OK, let's roll." He raised the hand-held mic to his face. "This is Will

Franklin on the Outer Banks of North Carolina. In one of the stranger stories of this storm, you can see a small boat headed out in these rough waters against all good judgment. It's hard to know what this lunatic is thinking…"

Will was so absorbed in the sensational nature of the shot that he hadn't noticed Sissy come into the camera shot just behind him on the other side. She reached him just as he declared that Duck was a "lunatic." In a rage, she snatched the microphone from his hand, drew back her arm, and threw it as far as she could into the churning, gray water. She turned on the reporter. Stepping toward him, an even wilder storm in her eyes, she yelled, "That's not a lunatic. That's a hero."

Startled, Will stumbled backward, his eyes wide with fear. As Sissy turned and strode off to her car, he watched, stunned. A moment later, he turned to the cameraman and asked, "Did you get all of that?"

Chapter 32

The bow of the boat jumped airborne and then banged down as gravity snatched it on the other side of the wave. The hull slammed down with a thud. Again, the wave, the flight, the drop, and the jolting impact. Over and over, the waves kept coming. Trista held on desperately as jolt after jolt she was thrown off balance. She'd tried the seat but found it too punishing, so she stood next to Duck, both hands grasping the boat, her legs acting as unsteady shock absorbers. Each crash of the bow threw up spray that could hardly be discerned in the drenching rain.

Trista looked down to the water rising on the deck at her feet. Before leaving the dock, Duck explained that the boat had a self-bailing system designed to siphon off any water that collected on the deck.

She yelled out over the wind and banging of the boat's hull, "Duck, I don't think self-bailing's working. The water's rising."

Completely engrossed in navigating the oncoming waves, Duck yelled, "It's working. It's just not designed to handle this much water."

"Then what good is it?"

Duck glanced over, but only briefly. "The longer we stay above water, the farther we can go. I'm just trying to get us there."

As the boat continued to jump and slam, Trista's concern grew. "Can this boat handle this abuse?"

Duck shouted, "She's a sturdy boat, but everything has its breaking point."

Trista thought, *everything... and everyone*. She wondered what would happen when the boat reached that point. Would it sink, leaving Duck and

Trista to drown, unnoticed specks in a vast ocean? Hadn't that already happened to each of them? She didn't know the details of Duck's disaster, but she assumed that, like her, he had been sailing along in a calm, sunlit existence. Then, some unexpected storm shattered everything, leaving each of them drowning in life's wind-swept seas. Once a boat goes down, there is no recovery. She wondered if they were beyond recovery. She turned to Duck and shouted, "Are you afraid?"

"Of what?" He glanced over quickly. "Dying?"

"Yes."

"Only a crazy person wouldn't be afraid of dying." There was a brief pause. He smiled. "I guess that's why it doesn't frighten me."

Trista placed her hand on his momentarily before grasping the boat again. "I don't think you're crazy. Only a brave man takes on an insane task like this."

Duck shouted above the wind, "You know what does frighten me?" Out of the corner of his eye, he saw her shake her head. He continued, "Letting you down."

Trista responded loudly, "I don't think you'll let me down." She looked at Duck's determined face. Just days earlier, she wouldn't have said this, but here he was, where no one else would go, on a task that must seem crazy, with a woman he barely knew.

He let out a deep sigh. "You don't know me well enough to say that. I am very capable of failing you."

Trista began to worry. There was no margin for error. She needed the determined Duck, not the self-doubting one. She said firmly, "I'm counting on you."

He shouted back, "Don't worry. I won't abandon you." Although she thought the remark was a bit odd, she was comforted by the determination in his voice.

They continued on, bouncing and crashing over the waves. The boat shuttered beneath their feet. Trista broke the silence. "As bad as this is, I thought it would be worse."

After a long moment, he shouted, "It will be… when we pass through the inlet into open water."

Trista looked down at the water growing deeper on the deck. She felt the banging of the hull as it slammed down after each crest. She wondered if open water would be that breaking point that Duck mentioned. She hoped that Jimbo was right, that if you had to be out in a hurricane, you would want Duck by your side. Quietly, she said, "Don't be afraid, Angie. I'm coming, baby."

At times, it seemed as if they were engulfed in a gray shroud of spray and wind-driven rain, unable to see beyond the current punishing wave. Occasionally, a ghastly smear of red would flash just to their left as one of the channel markers loomed out of the mist. Trista wasn't sure how Duck was able to navigate in these blinding conditions. She hoped that he knew where they were going.

After what seemed like forever, Trista strained to identify something large looming through the rain and spray. Just as she was able to make out the shape of a huge arching bridge, Duck shouted out, "We've made it to the inlet." Trista braced herself for the deteriorating conditions that Duck predicted, but even their violent roller coaster ride to this point didn't prepare her for what she saw. Past the bridge, an undulating, writhing monster named Renee lay in wait for the tiny craft. The huge waves dwarfed the small boat. Trista's heart dropped. What had Duck said? "They're all just specks in the ocean." At that moment, she wished that she were on a slightly bigger speck.

Chapter 33

The windshield wipers slapped frantically with little effect. Sissy could see only feet ahead of the jeep. Crawling south along Highway 12 at her current speed would probably put her at Oregon Inlet after Duck and Trista passed under the Bonner Bridge, but she still hoped to make it in time to catch a glimpse of them as they passed into the open water of the Atlantic. Judging from the downpour, she might not be able to see anything except rain. She pushed ahead, almost running off the road several times, being pulled by ponding water along the narrower stretches in the national park.

She tried to calm herself. If anyone could pull this off, it would be Duck. But what if it was impossible. She knew all too well that the "perfect" Duck wasn't. What if he failed? Suddenly, she would rather have broken, haunted Duck, alive, than the old confident Duck, dead. As she drove, she made herself repeat, over and over, "Duck can do this." Each mile that she traveled with the silent VHF radio sitting next to her gave her hope.

She felt that her best vantage point would be from Pea Island on the other side of the bridge. However, the thick sheets of rain obscured her view and the blasts of unobstructed wind made navigating the bridge difficult. Keeping the jeep between the lines was almost impossible. Luckily, there were no other cars on the highway.

She arrived at the other side of the inlet with little expectation that she would see the small boat. Horizontal sheets of rain obscured anything more than a few feet away. She pulled up the hood of her rain jacket and stepped out of the car. Sissy struggled against the wind gusts to draw closer to the shore. It was hopeless. She retreated to the shelter of the car.

Just as she slammed the door, the radio on the seat came alive with static and then the voice.

"MAYDAY, MAYDAY, MAYDAY

This is the *Second Chance, Second Chance, Second Chance*

Mayday this is the *Second Chance.*"

Even through the static, she recognized Duck's voice. It was surreal to hear him calmly issuing a distress call in the middle of the raging wind and rain. She listened for the location and was amazed to hear him give the map coordinates of the *Seamist's* accident. How were they able to get there so quickly in this nightmare of a storm? Duck's voice continued.

"Partially submerged and taking on water in heavy seas

We need emergency evacuation.

There are two adults on board.

The *Second Chance* is a twenty-four-foot sport-fishing vessel.

Over"

A second calm voice, not Duck's, broke in.

"Second Chance

Second Chance

This is Coast Guard Station Elizabeth City

We copy your location and have a helicopter in route.

Over"

Duck's voice, again calm, announced,

"Roger, Coast Guard Station."

Sissy had anticipated the worst and knew that, in the event of a Coast Guard rescue, they would be taken to the hospital in Elizabeth City for observation and treatment. She turned the key in the ignition and swung the car onto Highway 12 headed back over the bridge crossing the inlet. In one of the lulls between rain bands, the wind subsided to a mere drizzle. Sissy looked out toward the ocean. Through the gray haze of rain and mist, she could just make out the huge, rolling swells. As she turned back to the road, something caught her eye. Looking back, she saw a small boat rush up the face of a swell. Reaching the peak, the bow lunged out of the water, almost vertical. Quickly it came crashing down, disappearing behind the swell. Sissy stopped the car. There was no other traffic on the bridge. She watched again as the little boat rushed into view from the trough and crested, again becoming semi-airborne before crashing down and disappearing. Just then, the next torrent of rain and wind assaulted the car. The waves and boat disappeared. Hopelessly, she waited several minutes for the rain to subside. Sissy knew that she needed to get to the hospital. Reluctantly, she put the car in gear.

As she inched along the highway, hoping to find the road and not the bridge railings, she was troubled. That boat must have been Duck. Who else would be out in conditions like this? But that was not the location that he noted in his Mayday call. Was he lost? Was the navigational equipment malfunctioning? Would the Coast Guard be able to locate the boat? Sissy drove on through the rain, worried that there might not be anyone in the returning helicopter. Bad coordinates only make matters worse when you're just a speck in the ocean.

Chapter 34

As the bow of the small boat slipped up the face of the towering swell, Trista's feet were swept from under her by gravity and the ankle-deep water that now rushed toward the stern of the boat. She clung to the metal cockpit rails trying to keep from being washed toward the back of the boat. Before she could get her feet planted beneath her, the bow of the boat went airborne as it crested the swell. Crashing down on the backside, it sent water spraying into the boat. The impact of the landing and the rush of water caused her to lose her grip, and she slammed into the side of the cockpit, sending a shooting pain through her ribs.

Duck struggled to remain standing and in control of the wheel. He called out over the wind and waves, "Are you OK?"

Trista regained her grasp on the wet metal bars. "I'm good." She lied. Her ribs ached, and a searing pain seized her left knee. She'd probably twisted it trying to stay on her feet during that last wash.

Duck focused on the next approaching swell.

Trista called out, "We're not there yet, are we?"

"No." Watching the rising swell closely, Duck couldn't see the look of concern on Trista's face. As the bow of the boat rose, he called out, "Hold on."

Trista was prepared this time and adjusted her grip and placement of her feet so that she was more in the attitude of someone on a surfboard. She managed to keep her footing during the ascent, but still stumbled on the following crash. Still, in all, she handled it much better.

That swell past, she had just moments to be concerned. Something wasn't right about the Mayday call. She wondered if she had made a mistake trusting Duck. Maybe, as others thought, he *was* "a little off."

Trista shouted out with the next swell approaching. "Why did you give the Coast Guard the wrong map coordinates?"

A wry smile swept across Duck's face as he turned the boat into the next wave, taking it at a slight angle. The boat slid up the face. Trista braced herself as the boat went semi-airborne and crashed down, sliding into the trough.

Duck shouted over his shoulder. "What makes you think they were the wrong coordinates?"

Trista's concern rose even more. "Those are the coordinates where the *Seamist* sank. You said we're not there yet."

Duck continued to smile. "I gave them the right location. It's going to take a Coast Guard helicopter fifty minutes to reach that site. We'll be there before then."

The next swell was on them, and both of them focused on staying upright through the wild roller coaster action. The bow came down harder than the last time, sending a wash of water onto the deck. The water was getting deeper around their feet.

Duck continued, "We'll be there… if we don't lose the boat first. I'm just giving the Coast Guard a head start. I call it, 'just in time rescue.'" He was trying to lighten the mood in the face of their desperate situation. The boat was taking on water faster than the self-bailing system could spew it out. The hull of the boat was suffering much more punishment than it was designed to handle. Duck would do everything he could to get them to the site, but he had no control over the sea. The small boat was running like a rodent in a sadistic game of cat and mouse. Huge claws of water threw the boat in the air, letting it run for just a moment before snatching it and tossing it up again. It was all fun and games for the cat. But when the cat tired of the game, it never ended well for the mouse. Duck feared that would also be the fate of the tiny boat… and its passengers. He just didn't know when this monster cat would tire of the game.

The next swell was rushing toward them. Trista braced herself for the next flight and free-fall. She grasped the metal rails tightly, but she was weary. Her ribs ached with every move and her knee was beginning to throb. She had never run a marathon, but she imagined that this was what it must feel like to be one mile from the finish line – completely exhausted, to the point that standing was a struggle. Trudging along, putting one foot in front of the other, knowing that you've come too far to quit, and you've expended too much effort to run any farther. Like a marathoner, she would press on.

Just as the boat was launched from the top of the swell, the radio crackled.

> "Disabled vessel, *Second Chance*
>
> Disabled vessel, *Second Chance*
>
> This is Coast Guard Search and Rescue.
>
> We are en route to your location.
>
> Estimated arrival in forty—"

As the bow slammed down, water rushed over the console and the radio went dead. Now in the trough between waves, Duck tried to hail the Coast Guard rescue helicopter, but there was no response. He tried other channels without any luck and then came back to channel 16. Again, no response. The radio was dead.

Chapter 35

The helicopter cut through the heavy rain, flying east. Lieutenant Commander Rob Mitchell headed the chopper into the teeth of the wind and rain. He had years of experience in search and rescue and was very familiar with storm rescue off the Carolina coast. His crewmembers were not as experienced. His co-pilot, Lieutenant Steve Collins had only been flying search and rescue for about sixteen months. Their rescue technician, David Barnes, had seen only a few missions since transferring in six months ago. Mark Butler, their rescue swimmer, was brand new. This would be his first non-training hoist. These were not the best conditions to get your first experience as a rescue swimmer, but then no conditions were the best.

When hope was swept away with each crashing wave, and everything had gone to hell, boaters called on Coast Guard Search and Rescue. It was their job to fly into that hell and snatch the hopeless from the jaws of death. It never ceased to amaze Rob that in the middle of huge storms, this small craft with its four orange clad crewmembers represented salvation.

Lieutenant Collins tried raising the *Second Chance* on channel 16.

"Disabled vessel, *Second Chance*

Disabled vessel, *Second Chance*

This is Coast Guard search and rescue.

We are en route to your location.

Estimated arrival in forty minutes

Do you copy?"

He waited for a response. There was none. He repeated the message again with the same result. He switched over to channel 22, same message, same result.

There was a quiet moment in the cabin of the chopper. Collins spoke hopefully, "Their radio could be dead."

There was another brief silence before Rob spoke. "I've got a bad feeling about this one. It's Déjà vu for me."

"What do you mean?" Collins questioned.

"It was before any of you were stationed at Elizabeth City." Rob paused. "Exactly five years ago today… exactly to the day. We responded to a Mayday from a sinking forty-foot charter boat. They had been caught in a nasty nor'easter. When we arrived, the boat was in pieces and sinking. There were two people in the water, and we knew at least one person was missing. We came back empty. We lost them all." Rob became silent.

After a second, Collins spoke consolingly. "That's tough, but the same day is just a coincidence."

Rob interrupted, "The same day *and* the exact same map coordinates. I tell you I have a bad feeling about this one."

Mark, the new rescue swimmer, blurted out. "The same map coordinates? How do you even remember that after five years?"

Rob responded, "You're too new to know yet, but you remember the bad ones, every detail. It's etched in your brain. They play out like a horror film marathon in your dreams." He paused for a moment as if considering his next statement and then continued. "The blessing of what we do is that we save people's lives. The curse is that we don't save them all. Unfortunately, those are the ones that haunt you."

176

The cabin fell silent as the four men weighed the heavy responsibility that they carried. As the rain pounded down and the wind wailed, the chopper continued its flight into hell.

Chapter 36

Duck stole quick glances at the instruments as the *Second Chance* slammed down the backside of another wave. "Get ready. We're almost there," he shouted above the roar of the waves and wind. He wasn't sure what Trista had in mind. The effort of just getting them to this point had consumed all of his attention. He didn't know what he was telling her to get ready for. He knew that they wouldn't have long. Water almost filled the deck area and the cabin. They had been lucky just to get through the last couple of swells.

Holding on against the rolling action of the boat and wind with one hand, Trista removed the neoprene pouch containing the treasured necklace. She hesitated. To remove the necklace, she would need to use both hands, but the action of the boat was wild and unpredictable. She thought that she might just send the necklace to the bottom in the case, but she worried that it might hold air and float off. She tentatively released her grip on the boat and began to pry open the Velcro. Just then, the boat rolled hard, and her feet went out from under her. As she fell, Duck released the wheel of the boat, managing to grab at her arm and waist. He broke her fall, but not before her head struck the console. Immediately, the water around him was filled with blood and a steady stream of red ran down her face.

"Trista!" Duck cradled her in his arms, holding her above the water filling the deck. "Trista!" There was no response. He put his fingers to her neck, looking for a pulse. The rolling of the boat made it difficult, but he thought he felt one. She was alive but unconscious and losing blood quickly. Duck responded, grabbing the floating neoprene pouch and using it to apply pressure to the laceration.

With Duck away from the wheel, the boat drifted parallel to the next oncoming wave. The rushing swell lifted the boat sideways and rolled it violently, throwing Duck and Trista into the ocean. The boat came crashing, keel side up, into the water just beyond Duck. Very little of the boat could be seen above the thrashing waves.

Duck looked around for Trista but couldn't find her. He knew that the flotation vest would keep her head above water, but he needed to find her quickly. Her chances of surviving unconscious weren't good. Then he panicked. Could she be trapped under the boat? He dove below the surface, searching frantically beneath the almost submerged boat. It was a bit more difficult because of the life vest that he wore, but he managed to get under long enough to end his concern. As he broke the surface, he began swimming around the boat, looking for Trista on the other side. As he rounded the bow, he saw her orange vest, bobbing in the waves. After a few strong strokes, he was even with her and grabbed onto her vest. She was still unconscious. There was a jagged laceration on the side of her head, flooding the water around her, turning it a dark grayish red. Duck applied the neoprene pouch with his hand, attempting to stem the flow of blood, but the violent wave action made it difficult for him to keep steady pressure on the wound. She needed medical attention soon.

For what seemed like eternity, Duck clung to Trista. The unpredictable waves crashed over them. Duck covered her as best he could to keep her from breathing in the water. The wind and the waves clawed and pulled at the two, sometimes dragging them in different directions. Still, Duck held on. The muscles in his arms burned, and his fingers began to cramp, but he held on to Trista.

Just as he thought that he might not be able to hold on much longer, he heard the sound of rotors above the wail of the wind. Looking upward, he could just make out the lights of a helicopter emerging from the wind-driven rain. As the chopper hovered overhead, Duck allowed Trista to move away from him, still in his grasp. He motioned to her lifeless form floating in the orange vest. He was hoping that they would be able to tell that she was unconscious.

Soon Mark Butler, brand new rescue swimmer in his orange and yellow swimmer's dry suit, appeared and moved into a sitting position in the doorway. Duck watched as they lowered him near the two floating survivors. Duck swam toward the descending rescuer, dragging Trista behind him. As Mark neared the water, Duck yelled out as loud as he could, "She's unconscious."

The rescue swimmer was now in the water and signaled to the crew above that he was OK. Duck swam toward him, calling out, "She's unconscious and lost lots of blood. She needs medical attention."

Mark spoke above the roar of the rotors and the wind. "Right. I'll take her up with me first. Then I'll be back with a basket for you. Are you OK?"

"Yeah, I'm good. Just take care of her."

Duck held Trista as Mark strapped her for the hoist with him to the helicopter. As they made their slow ascent to the chopper, David steadied the hoist cable.

Collins' voice cut in, "Increase altitude. There's a big swell at three o'clock."

Rob quickly brought the helicopter up to a safe distance. David pulled Trista into the cabin followed by Mark. As the copter came about to locate Duck, David and Mark grimaced. They watched the *Second Chance,* in the throes of a huge wave, tumbled, tossed, and then splintered like dry balsa wood. They searched for the man in the orange life vest that they'd left below. David pointed, "There at five o'clock." The orange vest bobbed in the undulating water, but there was no one in it. The helicopter made several passes, as they tried desperately to find the remaining survivor. They found only pieces of the broken boat.

At this point, Mark was monitoring Trista's vital signs. "She's still unconscious. I've managed to slow the bleeding, but I think she's lost a lot of blood, and her pressure is dropping. We need to get her to a hospital."

Rob asked, "What do you think, Collins?"

"If he was still out there, we would've seen him by now. Without the life vest, he's probably gone. It's better to save one than to lose two. Let's get her to an emergency room."

Rob nodded, "Agreed. Let the hospital know we are en route."

Collins responded, "Roger," as the helicopter swung toward the west.

Chapter 37

Trista heard a voice calling through the thick mist. A figure floated toward her through the haze. As the figure drew closer, she could make out a white flowing gown dancing in the wind. It was a young girl, her long hair also moving in the breeze. The girl floated before her with outstretched arms that reached toward Trista. As the figure grew ever nearer, Trista heard the voice calling clearly, "Mommy. Where are you, Mommy?" She could now see the face of the young girl. It was her nine-year-old daughter, Angie. She floated in the mist, wearing her white baptismal day dress. Trista caught a glint of silver from her daughter's neck. The necklace. The other half of the heart necklace gleamed through the mist. Angie pleaded again, "Mommy. Where are you, Mommy?"

Unlike every time in the past, her daughter continued floating closer and closer, reaching out with open arms. Drawing ever nearer, she slowly transformed, becoming a tween and then a young teen. As she drew within a few feet, Trista could see that her fourteen-year-old Angie's dress and hair were not blowing in the wind. Rather, they were moving rhythmically with the ocean current.

Angie smiled, "Mommy, you came for me. I've been so lost without you."

Mother and daughter embraced. Holding her daughter tightly, Trista felt chills and a deep warmth all at the same time. Angie whispered, "Mommy, I will always love you."

Suddenly, there was blindingly bright light that surrounded her and seemed to fill the universe. Trista could see nothing but a light that was so brilliant that it hurt. Was this heaven? She must be in heaven. But where was Angie? She called out, "Angie, where are you? Angie, I love you too."

Like an eclipse of the sun, a dark shapeless object moved between Trista and the light. She became frightened. What was this dark figure? Where was Angie? Then an echoing, muffled voice called out, "Trista… Trista." Was God calling her name?

As her eyes began to focus, she could faintly make out bright fluorescent lights in the ceiling above where she lay. Still struggling to focus, she now recognized the blurred silhouette of someone standing over her, calling her name. She had difficulty seeing the face clearly. The voice sounded familiar. Who was it? "Trista… Trista. It's me… Sissy. Can you hear me?"

Sissy? She knew Sissy. She was still having trouble focusing on the face. It was mostly a blur. "Where's Angie?"

A nurse who'd just hurried into the room looked questioningly at Trista. She whispered to Sissy, "Was Angie on the boat?"

Sissy shook her head and whispered, "Her daughter, killed in a boating accident five years ago."

The nurse nodded in acknowledgment. Working in the emergency room had hardened her to the tragedies of life that played out there daily.

Trista continued to ask for Angie. Sissy spoke up, "Trista, you're in the emergency room. Do you remember going out in the boat?"

Trista looked at Sissy. Her vision was clearing but her thoughts were still very fuzzy. "Boat?"

"Yes, in the storm." Sissy was trying to ease her into the present.

Trista's face was blank. "Boat… in a storm." She looked off into the distance as if the answer were out there somewhere past the fluorescent lights above her. "Boat… the waves were huge." She reached up slowly and touched the place where the half-heart necklace once hung. "We were headed to the site of the accident."

Sissy could see her straining to clear the remaining cobwebs in her brain.

"Duck told me to get ready." Trista looked around the room. "Where's Duck?"

Sissy bit her lip and tried blinking away the tears as she looked away. She didn't want to cry. She managed to force it down as she turned back to face Trista.

Trista's voice rose with concern. "Where's Duck?"

Sissy just shook her head, unable to control the tears that now ran down her cheeks.

Trista became more agitated. "He made it, didn't he?"

Sissy shook her head again and sniffling said, "No, you're the only person the Coast Guard brought in."

Trista had only known him for days. She was surprised by the overwhelming sense of loss that she felt. The two women became one in the tears of loss that quietly streamed down their faces.

Wiping the tears with both hands, Trista sobbed, "It's all my fault. I'm sorry, Sissy. I should've told him I wouldn't go with him."

Sissy shook her head. "It's not your fault."

"Sure, it is. I kept pushing and pushing, raising the amount I offered to pay. It's all my fault."

"He didn't do it for the money."

Trista shook her head, her tears of sorrow mixed with tears of self-anger. "He knew it was suicidal to go out in that storm. Why else would he do it?"

Sissy stood silently, looking incredulously at Trista. "He didn't tell you, did he?"

Trista swiped angrily at her tears. "Didn't tell me what?"

"I can't believe that he didn't tell you. No… no, I can believe it. That poor, suffering, hardheaded…" Sissy shook her head. "He didn't tell you about the accident?"

Trista's tears trickled down her cheeks. "Well, he did… a little. Not a lot of details. He didn't tell me about his best friend dying or anything."

Sissy's eyes narrowed. "Really, what did he tell you?"

"Well, he told me that he had totaled his car. He didn't go into any more details, and you said that he didn't like to talk about it so…" Trista stopped, looking confused, as Sissy broke out into sad laughter.

Sissy drew in a deep breath. "That accident didn't kill anything except Duck's chances of driving for a while."

Trista looked confused.

"Well, I guess he left the story for me to tell." Sissy exhaled and then began. "After high school, Duck could have gone into a number of colleges on a competitive swimming scholarship. He was that good. Instead, he chose the Coast Guard. He wanted more than anything to use his talents to help others. He figured the best way to do that would be as a Coast Guard rescue swimmer. He was accepted into the program and not only survived but even thrived in one of the most demanding and rigorous training programs the military has. After graduation, he was assigned to Atlantic City, NJ. As our mother's health deteriorated, he somehow was able to swing a transfer to Elizabeth City so that he could be within driving distance." Sissy paused to study Trista who was looking at her cautiously, still a bit lost.

Now came the difficult part. Sissy started up again. "Five years ago, today. Duck's search and rescue team responded to a Mayday call from a forty-foot charter boat off the coast of North Carolina. The boat was being hammered by big waves and was taking on water." She looked at Trista whose eyes were wide with surprise. "That boat was the *Seamist*."

Trista looked lost. She blinked in disbelief as she searched around the room as if trying to find an answer on the walls. "But... I don't understand... He said... " She sat speechless for a long time and then looked back at Sissy. "I'm sorry but I never asked... What's your last name?"

Sissy said quietly, "Mallory."

Trista nodded her head slowly, her lips pursed. "And Duck's given name is?"

Sissy replied, "Jason... Jason Mallory."

Still lost, Trista blinked as if to clear blurred vision. "But Duck told me that Jason Mallory was dead. What did he say? Boating accident? Went down and never came up?" Then her face contorted in realization.

Sissy said, "He was never the same after that. Couldn't handle rescue missions. In fact, he couldn't handle much of anything. He went through counseling, but he couldn't let it go. He was eventually released from the Coast Guard. I took him back in with me, and I've been watching over him ever since. The Jason Mallory that I grew up with didn't come back... until yesterday."

"But why didn't he tell me?"

A twisted smile crept across Sissy's face. "He thought that you would blame him for your daughter's death, for his failure to save her."

"That's crazy. Why would he think that?" Trista asked, eyes wide, dumbfounded.

"Well, that's all he's heard for the past five years. People blamed him for his best friend Brody's death."

Trista sat, mouth open. "I still don't get it."

Sissy began the story again. "When the rescue helicopter arrived at the site, the *Seamist* was in bad shape. The hull had cracked and split open. It was only holding together along one side of the hull. Duck said it looked like the flap of a cardboard box flexing and twisting in the huge waves. It was upside down in the water and mostly submerged. Air pockets trapped beneath it were probably the only thing keeping it barely afloat. From the helicopter, Duck could see two people in life vests in the water. The Mayday call indicated there were three people on the boat, but the rescue crew never saw the third person.

As Duck was being lowered to the water, a wave crashed over the boat and the survivors. The hull of the boat split completely. As the swell subsided, one life vest surfaced off the bow and another about forty yards away, off the stern. He was being lowered nearest the one at the stern. Duck swam to the life vest and found that it was his best friend Brody, who had been captain of the family boat *Seamist* that day. Brody told Duck to save the girl near the bow of the boat first. She was panicked and hysterical. Duck knew that Brody was a very good swimmer. Almost as good as Duck. He felt confident that saving the girl first was the right choice. As he swam toward her, another wave crushed down on them. The bow of the boat flipped and then sank quickly as he swam past it. A second wave crashed over Duck and the girl. As he emerged from the water, the girl was gone. He looked around frantically but couldn't find her. He dove and could barely make out her orange vest below the surface. As he dove deeper, he closed in on her. Seeing him, she reached out. His hand was within inches of hers when she was swept away by the rushing water. He continued to swim deeper but couldn't find her. Gasping for air, he returned to the surface, horrified to find that the stern of the boat was gone and so was Brody. He dove time and again, trying to find the girl or Brody but came up empty. Finally, exhausted, he was hoisted to the helicopter. Back in the cabin, he learned that a wave had picked up the stern and slammed it down on top of Brody, dragging him to the bottom as it sank." Sissy stopped, eyes closed, completely spent from telling the story.

Trista sat with tears streaming down her cheeks. "But why do they blame Duck for Brody's death?"

Sissy sighed. "People who were close to Brody didn't understand how Duck could abandon his best friend to save a…" Sissy's voice trailed off, realizing that she had said too much.

Trista finished the sentence. "to save a stranger. I get it now."

Sissy looked down at the floor in shame. Quietly, she said, "I'm sorry."

The awkward silence in the room became suffocating.

Sissy stared absently off toward the nurses' station just outside the glass wall of Trista's small emergency room. She sat in the room but was off somewhere else in the past. She barely noticed the man in the orange flight suit studying her as he strode past. A second later, he stepped back into the doorway. "Sissy?"

Sissy's eyes shot up to see Rob Mitchell standing in the doorway.

Rob looked surprised to see her. "What are you doing here?"

Sissy broke down. "Duck's gone, Rob."

Rob glanced nervously down the hall and then back at Sissy. "What do you mean, 'Gone?'"

"He's gone, not coming back."

Rob's eyes narrowed. "I don't understand."

Sissy pointed to Trista. "She was on the boat with him today when it went down, but they didn't bring him back." Sissy began sobbing uncontrollably.

Rob's confused expression melted, "I know. I'm the one who flew her here."

Startled, Sissy glanced up. Her sobbing subsided.

"And it would take more than a tropical cyclone to kill that lunkhead brother of yours. We just made our second trip out there to fish him out of the ocean." A smile swept across Rob's face. He pointed down the hall. "He's in the room at the end of the hall, mostly in one piece."

Both women sat speechless.

"He's pretty beat up from the waves. He spent quite a bit of time in the water since he decided not to catch the first ride."

Sissy jumped to her feet and grabbed Rob, hugging him tightly as she said over and over, "Thank you, thank you, thank you."

As she released Rob, she realized that there was an introduction she needed to make. "Rob, this is Trista. Trista, this is Lieutenant Commander Rob Mitchell. He was the pilot of the rescue helicopter that responded to the *Seamist* Mayday call." Motioning, Sissy explained, "Trista's daughter was on the *Seamist*."

As Rob shook her hand, he was consoling, "I'm really sorry, ma'am."

Trista shook her head. "You've got nothing to be sorry for. I want to thank you for risking your life for my daughter and for me… and for Duck."

Rob chuckled and looked over at Sissy, "Well, you can tell that brother of yours that if he decides to go scuba diving in a hurricane again, he won't have to worry about the storm. I'll kill him myself." Rob smiled and winked. Then he became serious. "Look, Sissy, I won't pretend to understand what he was doing out there today, but," nodding toward Trista, "I certainly understand why."

A voice down the hall called to Rob. "Well, I gotta go. It's a busy day. Tell Duck to stay safe and give me a call sometime. I miss the guy."

As he turned to leave, Sissy called out, "Wait!" Rob turned back. Sissy's face looked like one engrossed in assembling one of those thousand-piece puzzles. "What made you fly back out?"

Rob smiled and shook his head. "About the time we landed at the hospital with your friend," motioning toward Trista, "we got a distress signal from a PLB. It led us to Duck not far from where we found her."

Rob could almost hear the gears grinding in Sissy's head. Another call from down the hallway and he declared, "I've really gotta go." He waved as he strode off down the hall.

Trista and Sissy looked at each other and simultaneously exclaimed, "Scuba diving?"

Then Trista, looking confused, asked, "What's a PL-whatever?"

Sissy chuckled, an edge of annoyance in her tone. "A PLB? It's a personal locator beacon for emergencies. Works kinda like a GPS, leading rescue teams to stranded individuals. Duck had one that he kept in a dive-safe canister." Lips pursed and eyes ablaze, Sissy muttered, "Move over Rob and Renee, 'cause I'll kill him myself."

Quietly, Trista suggested, "Maybe we should go see if he's alive before you decide to kill him." She shrugged and grinned.

Sissy couldn't keep a straight face. Her anger melted into a broad smile. "Come on, I'll give you a hand."

Sissy helped Trista out of bed, and they headed down the hall to find his room, Sissy on one side of Trista supporting her and the IV bag tree on the other. They moved down the hallway past the curious expressions of nurses and doctors.

Chapter 38

Duck appeared to be asleep, an IV in his arm and monitor leads strung from nearly every part of his body. Sissy and Trista approached the side of his bed. Sissy took his hand in hers. Duck's eyes barely opened. In a weak voice, he said, "Hey, Sis, what are you doing here?"

"Somebody told me that my brother had been scuba diving in a hurricane. I just had to see for myself."

Duck gave a feeble smile, "Guilty as charged." He noticed Trista standing just beyond his sister. "Who's this beautiful woman you brought with you?"

Trista blushed. "That boat ride today? You know how to show a girl a good time." She smiled.

Duck returned a weak smile.

Sissy became the serious older sister. "Scuba diving? Are you crazy?"

Duck objected, "Sis, don't bust my chops on this."

Sissy stood with arms crossed and a disapproving scowl.

Duck flashed a quick smile. "As they were hoisting Trista to the copter, I thought, I'm here – why not? So, I swam under the boat and slipped on my gear. Got out of there just as the boat got hammered. That was close."

Sissy's anger was beginning to rise. "In a hurricane?"

"Come on, Sis. Once you get down a few feet, you don't feel any effects of the wind. Fifty feet down, the *Seamist* was strangely calm below the crashing waves above."

Sissy continued the interrogation. "And you just *happened* to have your dive gear with you?"

Duck shrugged and smiled sheepishly.

"Look at you. You could have been killed."

"Look, Sis, I'm beat up from being above the water, not under it." He paused, changing the subject. "Hey, where's my stuff?"

Sissy searched around the small room and then opened the tiny closet. There, inside, was a plastic bag containing some of Duck's personal items."

He motioned to Sissy, "Bring it here."

With the bag sitting on his chest, he rummaged through it for a few seconds and then pulled a neoprene pouch from the bag.

Trista recognized the pouch, and her concern began to rise as he opened it, pulling out a sparkling chain. Dangling from the center of the chain was a shiny half-heart necklace with Trista's name engraved on one side. She cried out, "No, they were supposed to be together! No!"

Duck held up his hand to calm her. Then he reached into the bag again and drew out a gray-looking chain. Dangling from the center was the dull, tarnished other half-heart necklace. "I figured Angie would want you to keep both halves." He paused. "She's still down there if you want to give her a proper burial… I'll help."

Trista rushed toward Duck almost tripping over her IV tree. She bent down with tears in her eyes, hugged him tightly, and kissed his cheek. "Thank you," she exclaimed as she picked up the two necklaces. She placed them carefully side-by-side in the palm of her hand and silently read the inscription, *Mother – Daughter, Sharing One Heart*. Reverently, she slipped them on.

A passing nurse stopped in the doorway. "Ma'am, you need to return to your room. You can't be down here."

Sissy said, "Go ahead. I'll be back down there in a minute."

Trista hugged and kissed Duck again before wheeling her IV bag down the hallway to her room.

Alone with Duck now, Sissy's eyes narrowed. "How did you know that you would find the other half of the heart down there? Her daughter and the necklace should have washed away a long time ago."

Shaking his head, Duck said, "I didn't. I was just going to leave the necklace with the wreckage, but when I got to it, I discovered why I wasn't able to get to Angie that day. As the bow sank in the churning water, her leg somehow became entangled in the anchor line. The sinking bow dragged her down with it. You can imagine what five years in the water has done, but she's still there entangled in the line."

Sissy looked confused. "I still don't get it. If you weren't expecting to find the other half of the necklace, why dive to the wreckage? You could've just dropped Trista's necklace and hitched a ride on the copter the first time."

Duck winked and gave his sister a wry smile. "I went down looking for something else." He fished through the plastic bag lying on his chest and pulled out a dirty-looking chunk of clear plastic. It was about four inches square and about a half-inch thick. There appeared to be holes drilled in the four corners, perhaps for mounting. Duck asked Sissy to give him a few wet paper towels. Taking them, he scrubbed the surface for a moment and then held it up for her to see. In the center of the clear plastic was a gold medal emblazoned with the image of a swimmer and the words etched around the perimeter, "First Place – North Carolina State High School Athletic Association Championship."

Sissy gasped.

"Yeah, Brody had it encased in plastic and then mounted it on the console of the *Seamist*. You know, that race was the only time I can remember seeing Brody's father show any pride in his younger son. I can't bring Brody back, but I can give his father this."

Sissy sat dumbfounded, unable to speak. First, Duck tackled the hurricane and now he would face Brody's family. If anyone ever doubted Duck's courage, this should end that doubt.

Chapter 39

The sun was just beginning to rise as they left the hospital parking lot in Sissy's jeep, headed east toward the Outer Banks. Trista and Duck had both been given a clean bill of health and released. Except for feeling a bit weak, Duck was in good shape. Trista, stitches in her scalp and an ace bandage on her knee, was otherwise OK.

It was hard to believe that just twenty-four hours earlier, eastern North Carolina was being lashed by blustery winds and heavy rain. Where yesterday's horizon was gray and foreboding, today's glowed with streaks of red and orange giving way to the yellow of a bright, shining sun. The long, ragged clouds above formed bright red gashes in the already blue sky. In moments, they would be gone.

After driving for a while, Sissy turned to Duck. "Back at the hospital... before we knew that you were still alive... I told Trista the story."

Duck turned toward his sister, glaring. "Story? Which Story?"

Sissy, her eyes back on the road, hands gripping the wheel, spoke. "You know. A storm tossed, sinking ship. Two people in trouble. A courageous rescue swimmer desperately trying but unable to save them."

Trista saw Duck wince just before he looked away from his sister and out the side window of the car. She reached forward laying her hand on his shoulder. She spoke quietly, "Thank you, Duck." She could see his pained expression reflected in the glass.

"Thanks? For what? Failing to save your daughter?" She detected a slight quiver in his voice.

"No. I want to thank you for risking your life to save a little girl you didn't even know." Except for the humming sound of the tires on the road, the car was silent for a long moment. Then she spoke again. "Yesterday, in the boat, you told me your greatest fear was failing me. Well, you didn't fail me yesterday… and you didn't fail me five years ago."

As Duck stared out at the passing landscape, and the car drove on in silence, Trista ran her hand lightly across the back of his shoulder.

To end the awkward silence, Sissy turned on the radio and tuned it to a station that was reporting on the aftermath of the storm. The upper-level wind shear had reduced the hurricane to a tropical storm as it blew out to sea, never making landfall. Portions of the Outer Banks were still without power, but the flooding had been much less than anticipated and damage to buildings was minimal. Most of the news was good. It was very likely that they would return to a cottage and not a pile of rubble.

As the news report droned on, Sissy looked over and Duck, exhausted, was slumped against the window asleep. She looked back in the mirror. There was no Trista. Glancing over her shoulder, Sissy could see her lying across the back seat, also asleep. She drove on in silence, her thoughts spinning from amazement, to gratitude, to concern – round and round emotions swirled in her heart.

The signs of the storm became more apparent with each passing mile. There were downed trees by the side of the road. Occasionally, large limbs blocked one of the lanes. Clean-up crews worked to remove debris from the highway and power lines.

Approaching the bridge leading into the Outer Banks, Sissy began to feel anxious. She knew Duck wanted to take care of the medal as soon as possible. She woke the two sleeping passengers.

Glancing at Trista in the mirror, Sissy said, "Back at the hospital, I told you about Duck's friend Brody. Well, Duck retrieved something from the wreckage that he wants to return to Brody's father. We'll drop you at the cottage, and then Duck and I will take care of it."

Trista commented, "I'd like to tag along if you don't mind."

Given all the bad blood between the two families and Trista's connection to the family's lost boat, Sissy wasn't sure that it was a great idea. She glanced questioningly at Duck.

He shrugged, "Sure. Why not."

They stopped at their cottage only long enough to change out of their swimwear, the wetsuits having been cut away in the rush of emergency treatment. Pulling out of the drive, Duck looked back.

"The beach bunker seems to have weathered another storm." Duck winked at Sissy. She could tell that he was poking fun at himself and the comment he made just days earlier.

As they passed *The One That Got Away*, the café and marina looked normal, serene. However, signs of the storm could be seen along the narrow road. Debris and leaves had been washed over the highway and deposited on the asphalt as the water receded. Occasionally along the side of the road, unusual items sat, abandoned by the water. At one point, a doghouse sat upside down on the edge of the asphalt. A little farther on, Sissy swerved to miss a cooler that rested in the center of the road.

Beau lived with his father in a small cottage on a narrow road just off Highway 12. As they neared the home, Sissy noted the old pickup truck sitting in the drive. It was Beau's. More than likely that meant he was home. That would only make this more difficult. She pulled in behind the truck and parked. Duck, Sissy, and Trista exited the car and climbed the steps to the front deck. Duck hammered on the door.

In a moment, Beau opened it. Angrily, he shouted, "You've got a lot of nerve showing up here. Get off our property, you murdering little weasel."

Without flinching, Duck announced, "I'm here to see your father."

Beau bellowed, "Don't you get it? My father doesn't want to see you."

Duck remained calm. "Maybe, but why don't you let him tell me that."

Beau exploded. "Get out of here!"

Then from the darkness behind Beau, the old man's feeble voice called out, "Who is it, Beau?"

"It's a murdering son of a— "

"Is it Duck? Let him in."

"Pops!"

The old man's voice became more commanding. "I said let him in!"

Beau glared at Duck for a moment and then stepped back to let Duck through the door. Sissy and Trista followed closely behind.

The inside of the cottage was dark. Heavy drapes covered the windows, stifling all light from the outside. Everything seemed to be in disarray. Beer cans and whiskey bottles littered the floor and tabletops. Empty pizza boxes were piled haphazardly on a counter in the kitchen. This was even worse than Duck's mess. The old man sat at the kitchen table with a half-empty bottle of whiskey. As Duck stepped toward him, the old man threw back a shot, wiped his mouth with his sleeve, and then slammed the shot glass on the table.

Beau started up before Duck could speak. "Pops, we can't have this murderer—"

The old man slammed the palm of his hand on the table as he shouted, "Shut up, Beau. Let Duck say what he came to say."

Beau fell silent, but he was boiling inside.

Before Duck could speak, the old man looked up at him with bloodshot eyes glazed over from the booze. "I hear you got a death wish, out there in that storm."

Duck replied, "No, sir. Just went out there to bring you something back." He pulled the plastic encased gold medal from a bag and laid it on the table in front of the old man, who sat, working to make his eyes focus on the object. Then he reached out with a trembling hand. Lightly, he ran his fingers over the surface of the plastic as if he were touching a revered religious relic.

Tears trickled down the old man's face as he unexpectedly chuckled. "Brody bested you that day, didn't he?"

Quietly, Duck replied, "Yes, sir. He sure did. He bested me that day."

The old man continued to cry and chuckle as he stroked the medal.

Beau couldn't stay silent any longer. He growled, "Just because you bring in a worthless chunk of plastic—"

The old man shouted, "BEAU, SHUT UP!" It was with such unexpected force that the ensuing silence consumed the dark room. All stood shocked.

Quietly, almost timidly, Beau spoke up again. "But Brody's killer—"

The old man slammed his hand down loudly on the table again and rose shakily, turning toward Beau. "Brody's killer? What do you know about Brody's killer?" The old man sneered, "Nothing!"

Beau opened his mouth as if to speak but thinking better of it stood silent.

The old man continued. "Brody's killer? Well, it's certainly not Duck. He's risked his life twice for us. Is that a killer?"

Beau blurted out, "But he—"

The old man shouted, "Don't! Don't disrespect Duck that way. All he's ever done is sacrificed for others." He stood, pointing a bony finger at Beau. "Don't… you… dare!" He took a deep breath and stood up straight. "Brody's killer? You really want to know?" The old man looked each person in the room in the eye and then settled his hard glare on Beau. "I killed Brody."

Beau shouted out, "No, Pops, that's not true."

Still glaring, the old man shook his head. "Yes, it is. Brody didn't want to take that charter. He knew it wasn't safe. He flat out told me he wouldn't go." A slight drunken grin came across the old man's face. "But I knew how to make him. I couldn't force him, but I could make him." The old man giggled at this drunken memory. "I played him like a fiddle. I told him that if his brother Beau was here, he'd go out. Beau wasn't a coward. Hell, I even threatened to call Duck to see if he would come and take the boat out. Duck wasn't afraid of nothin'."

The room was as quiet as a tomb. Exhausted, the old man slumped back into the chair. "Yes sir, I played him good. Want to or not, he went."

In anguish, Beau pleaded, "Why, Pops? Why would you send him out in that storm?"

The old man turned angrily on Beau. "Because we needed the money!" Then wearily looking up at the ceiling as if to heaven he repeated, "We needed the money."

In amazement Beau muttered, "But we were OK when I left."

The old man spat out, "That's just it. You left." He sighed deeply. "I can fish, but I'm no businessman. The debts started piling up and then, just as things were looking really bad, this fool comes along offering twice the going rate for a charter." The old man broke down, sobbing, "You don't have to look far to find your brother's killer."

Duck placed his hand on the old man's shoulder to comfort him. "You didn't kill Brody. The sea did."

The old man's shoulders heaved as he sobbed.

"On this narrow strip of land, we're just her live-in lover. We live with her… and can't live without her. On sunny days, she sparkles. But let her have a bad day and, in one fitful rage, any of us could pay the price." As the old man continued to sob, Duck said quietly, "Maybe we should go."

As Duck headed toward the door, he stopped and turned back. "You're wrong, you know." The old man looked up at Duck through glazed eyes. "You didn't make Brody go. He always had a choice. He chose to go." Duck smiled as he glanced at Trista. "A friend once told me that only a brave man takes on an insane task. Brody was a brave man."

The old man nodded, now staring down at the gold medal on the table.

Duck stood for a moment longer and then said, "We should get back home."

As he walked toward the door with Trista and Sissy in tow, the old man called out, "Duck, thank you. Thank you for bringing a part of my boy back to me."

Duck turned and smiled, "No thanks necessary."

"Well, I disagree. I don't know how much you still owe on that old boat, but we're going to forgive the rest of the debt."

Beau began to wail, "No, Pops, don't. No, you can't."

Duck said, "Thank you, sir." He then turned and stepped out the door with Trista behind him.

As Sissy passed Beau, who was still wailing and holding his head with both hands, she stopped. Reaching into her pocket, she pulled out an envelope and slammed it into Beau's chest, knocking him off balance and sending him stumbling backwards. "Here's your damn money. I told you that you'd have it by Friday." The envelope fell to the floor and several hundred-dollar bills spilled out, scattering in the breeze from the doorway. Sissy strode out the screen door, letting it slam behind her.

As she stepped into the sunlight, she found Duck and Trista standing close to one another at the bottom of the steps. Duck looked up at the sky and exhaled deeply as Trista ran her hand consolingly along the back of his shoulders. Bounding down the stairs, Sissy said, "Let's get out of here."

After settling into the jeep, Sissy turned to Duck, her hand on the key. "You know, I watched every one of your swim meets growing up. You never lost except for that one." She pointed toward the cottage where the gold medal rested on the table. "You were ahead going into the final 10 meters." She paused, her eyes narrowed, studying Duck's face carefully. "You short-armed the last stroke, didn't you? You let Brody win."

Duck was silent for a moment, and Sissy could tell that he was carefully considering his answer. He exhaled audibly. "You know, Brody and I were best friends for years. I knew him better than anyone. Until that race, I never saw his father express even the slightest bit of pride in Brody's accomplishments. It was always Beau. Beau was stronger, faster, smarter." Duck chose his words carefully. "I think every child should feel their parent's pride and love. Don't you?"

Sissy waited for more, but Duck was quiet. She knew this would be as close to an answer as she would ever get.

In the back seat, Trista lovingly caressed the necklaces with her fingers, feeling the inscription engraved on the surface of each. She closed her eyes, and whispered to herself, "Yes, I do."

Chapter 40

Sissy nodded, turned the key, and swung the jeep down the road and out onto Highway 12, headed back toward their little cottage. They drove along in silence. Duck was the first to speak. "I'm exhausted."

Sissy glanced over, "You've got good reason to be."

Smiling, Duck commented, "I'm not sure which kicked my butt worse, the storm or trying to set things right with Brody's dad."

Sissy looked in the rearview mirror. Trista gazed out the side window, watching the shrubs and cottages flicker by. Sissy noticed that she absently ran her fingers over the two necklaces that she wore.

Sissy called back, "How're you doing back there?"

There was no response.

"Trista?"

Jerking around toward Sissy's voice, Trista blinked. "What's that?"

Sissy smiled. "Just wondered how you're doing."

A serene smile stole across Trista's face. "I'm good. Better than I've been in a long time."

Sissy glanced back again. "You just seemed so deep in thought."

Trista's smile grew wider. "I was just marveling how five years ago, in a single event, life threw strangers into the heart of a storm. All of us have been battered by the crashing waves ever since. And then in some wild twist of events, five years later, we're brought together so that another storm can deliver us. It's just… just…" She searched for the right word.

"Miraculous," Duck added.

"Yes, miraculous!" Trista exclaimed.

Just as they approached the marina, Duck noticed Jimbo dragging a chair out of the café onto the deck. "Hey, Sis, pull in. Let's give Jimbo a hand."

Sissy turned into the gravel lot, parking up near the deck. Jimbo, who was dragging a second chair through the door, stopped and stood watching the car. As Duck slid out of the passenger side, Jimbo's voice boomed, "Duck!" Neither Sissy nor Duck had ever seen Jimbo run in the past. But here was the big man, running awkwardly down the steps toward them, breathing heavily. He threw his arms around Duck, lifting him off the ground and swinging him around like a rag doll. "You're alive! I can't believe you're alive!"

Laughing and struggling, Duck yelled out, "Jimbo, stop! You're crushing me."

Jimbo let go, dropping Duck to the ground. "Man, when your boat was missing from the dock this morning, I was just sure that I would never see it or you again." Looking toward the end of the dock, Jimbo stopped. "Where's the boat?"

With his index finger pointing downward, Duck made a spiraling motion like water going down the drain.

Jimbo's eyes grew big as he gave out a low whistle. "But here *you* are." He glanced over at Trista. "You were on the boat?"

Trista slowly nodded her head.

Jimbo thought for a second and then, making eye contact with Trista, said, "What'd I tell you, huh? When things are bad, Duck's the man to have with you."

Trista smiled, cutting her eyes toward Duck, "You were right. He's the man to have with you." She wasn't sure, but she thought she detected a touch of crimson rising in Duck's face.

Trying hard to change the subject, Duck spoke. "Enough chit-chat. We actually stopped to help you get the café back into shape. So, let's make it happen." He clapped his hands together and bounded up the steps to press the issue. Trista and Sissy exchanged a knowing glance before following him up the stairs.

With the four of them working together, the plywood was quickly removed from the windows and the deck furniture was back in its usual place. Trista stood looking over the deck. It was as if there had never been a storm. Duck stepped out of the door and called to Trista, "Want to check out the marina?"

Turning, she grinned, "Sure."

Together they descended the wooden stairway and crossed the gravel lot to the boat slips.

Inside the café, Sissy carried boxes filled with napkin holders and salt and pepper shakers out of the storage closet. She began laying out the plaid, red-checked tablecloths and returning the service items to the tabletops. As she did, she worried. The same thought had dogged her on the drive all the way home from Elizabeth City. What was Duck going to do without the boat? She looked up and realized she didn't see Duck or Trista.

She called out to Jimbo in the back. "Have you seen Duck and Trista?"

Jimbo's voice came back, "Not in a while."

Sissy left her tables and wandered out onto the deck. No Duck or Trista.

She slipped down the stairs and across the lot. Reaching the foot of the dock, she saw the two standing at the other end where the *Second Chance* had once been moored. They stood with their backs toward her, facing the sound. Their arms were wrapped around each other's waists. Trista's head rested on Duck's shoulder.

Sissy smiled. It was then that she realized that Duck didn't need the boat anymore. In some mystical, unexpected way, the *Second Chance* had done exactly what her mother had intended. It gave Duck his life back, and in Trista's "miracle" did the same for her. She watched the couple clinging tightly to each other and thought how, like the necklaces, they were two torn and jagged hearts brought together and made one in the storm.

*   *   *   *   *

Thanks for reading *Hearts in the Storm.* If you enjoyed the story, please take a second to rate it. Help others find their next great read before moving on to your own new adventure.

Happy Reading,
Elmer

Acknowledgements

I would like to thank my beautiful wife, Mitzi, for all that she has done to make this novel possible. She has been my cheerleader, encouraging me during my frequent spells of self-doubt. On numerous occasions, she has been my sounding board, giving me insight into plot and characters. Her patience with my hours away as I wrote and rewrote this novel has been remarkable. She has truly been my inspiration.

I would also like to give a special thanks to Meagan Taylor-Booth for providing valuable feedback during revision of this novel.

The genesis of this story came from our rising high school senior. She expressed a desire to enter the Coast Guard after graduation. When we asked her why she was so interested in the Coast Guard, she said, "I want to help people." Out of that simple comment, the story was born as I walked the beach on vacation that summer.

This is a work of fiction. The characters, places, and events are either constructs of the author's imagination or used fictitiously. Any resemblance to real individuals, living or dead, events, or places is completely coincidental.

What is real, however, is the courage and dedication of the brave men and women of the United States Coast Guard Search and Rescue. I am not a "Coastie." What knowledge that I have comes from hours of research. I have tried to "get it right" in this novel. Unfortunately, research can never replace experience. If I have fallen short, I apologize. Please remember that it is, after all, a piece of fiction.

This book is dedicated to the men and women who willingly go into hell "so others may live." As Rob says in the novel, the job comes with a blessing and a curse. The blessing is that, in answer to desperate prayers, they save people's lives. The curse? Living with the realization that they're not able to save them all.

About the Author

Elmer Seward was born and raised along the Chesapeake Bay in southeast Virginia. When he was growing up, the cemetery behind his house was his playground. The metaphorical theme of death and rebirth that figures prominently in his novels is probably influenced in some way by the time that his mother heard, through the screened window, a small voice crying for help. Rushing from the house and through the yard, she discovered her all-too-curious six-year-old son at the bottom of a freshly dug grave. In that moment, he discovered that trouble is much easier to get into than it is to get out of. Sometimes we need help getting out of the hole that we jump into willingly.

He is blessed to have a large, blended family. He is also the reluctant servant to two crazy dogs, a Cocker Spaniel and a BruMaltChiYorkie. All of these strongly influence the characters and events in his novels; however, his beautiful wife, Mitzi, is the true inspiration for the tenderhearted but determined women in his stories.

Connect with Elmer

Follow Elmer and receive updates on his novels through the following social media.

Author Website: http://www.elmerseward.com

Facebook Page: https://www.facebook.com/ElmerSewardAuthor

Follow on Twitter: @elmerseward2

Other Books by Elmer Seward

Set You Free

Deena is running from a dangerous past. When she finds herself in a small fishing village tucked away on the banks of the Chesapeake Bay, she thinks she is finally safe. While there, she discovers a journal that weaves a story of secrets, passion, and unrequited love. In its pages, she discovers the answers to her struggle with the shadows of her own past. In the end, those shadows close in on her and threaten all that she holds dear.

Dreams of the Sleepless

Joe has been running for months, trying to escape the nightmares of his past. On a sleepless summer morning, he becomes entangled in the lives of Molly, a young woman who can no longer see a future, and Eli, an old man who wishes he could erase his past. A violent confrontation in those early hours with Jeb, Molly's cruel ex-boyfriend, explodes in events that will change all four lives.

After the Wanting

Rising Internet sensation or creepy-guy magnet? Rachel's life is a muddle of highs and lows. Just as her popular product review vlog is taking off, she finds herself fleeing to the seclusion of Virginia's Eastern Shore to escape her most recent romantic disaster. Lex's single-minded pursuit of Rachel frightens her.

To be loved and to be safe - That's all she wants.
But terror awaits... *After the Wanting*.

www.ingramcontent.com/pod-product-compliance
Lightning Source LLC
Chambersburg PA
CBHW070821120626
46556CB00002B/608